"YOU CAN COME OUT NOW."

Sniff.

There. He'd definitely heard something. There was a kid in the room. But where?

Matthew looked for hiding places. He crossed the room and reached for the closet doorknob.

"Did you ever hear your stepmom talk about her brother? That's me. You can call me Uncle Matt."

"Really?" a small voice asked.

The flowered tablecloth that covered the small bedside table shifted slightly. Matthew had the sudden feeling he was being scrutinized to see if he passed muster as uncle material.

"I'm Danny." A childish sigh echoed through the room. "Is the bogeyman gone?"

"Yeah, it's safe now."

The tablecloth rustled and the child bolted from his hiding place, launching himself into Matthew's arms. As the boy held tight, Matthew found himself murmuring all sorts of promises, especially the most important one: "I won't let anybody hurt you."

ABOUT THE AUTHOR

Born and raised in Birmingham, Alabama, Laura Kenner is a military wife and mother of two. A military assignment brought her to Colorado Springs, where she met a group of people who shared her passion for writing. She credits their support, instruction and friendship with helping her achieve her two greatest dreams within weeks of each other: selling her first book to Harlequin Intrigue, and winning the Romance Writers of America's Golden Heart Award. Laura loves to hear from readers, and can be reached at: P.O. Box 10055, Grand Forks AFB, ND 58204, or via E-mail at Connections at the Harlequin/Silhouette web site at: http://www.romance.net.

Books by Laura Kenner

HARLEQUIN INTRIGUE
263—SOMEONE TO WATCH OVER ME
313—A KILLER SMILE
405—HERO FOR HIRE

Through the Eyes of a Child
Laura Kenner

Harlequin Books

TORONTO • NEW YORK • LONDON
AMSTERDAM • PARIS • SYDNEY • HAMBURG
STOCKHOLM • ATHENS • TOKYO • MILAN
MADRID • WARSAW • BUDAPEST • AUCKLAND

To the students, faculty, alumni and friends of
The Altamont School, Brooke Hill School and
Birmingham University School, and to a fearless leader
among their ranks, the real Phoebe Robinson, whose
generosity of spirit is cherished by all.

And, as always, to the Wyrd Sisters, taskmasters,
brainstormers and best friends.

ISBN 0-373-22465-6

THROUGH THE EYES OF A CHILD

Copyright © 1998 by Laura Hayden

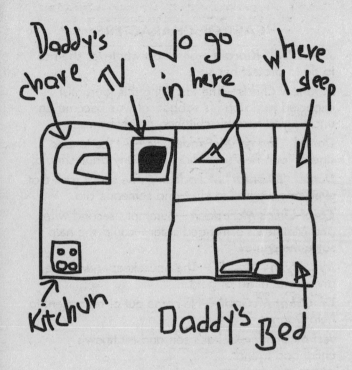

As drawn by Danny McFadden, age 4

CAST OF CHARACTERS

Jillian "Jill" Kincaid—She'll do whatever she has to do to protect her son.

Matthew Childs—The last thing this journalist expected to do on his sabbatical was become an uncle—and face his childhood nightmares.

Daniel "Danny" McFadden, Jr.—At the tender age of four, he's seen more than any adult should.

Daniel "Bummpt" McFadden—The shock jock that everyone wanted to kill—and someone did.

Carol Childs McFadden—Bummpt's second wife and Matthew's estranged sister—could she help solve the crime?

Mrs. Flynn "Mrs. F"—The housekeeper with the proverbial heart of gold.

Dr. Oskar McGrath—He came out of retirement to help Danny.

Jeff McGrath—Oskar's son and Matthew's childhood friend.

Sid McDonald—The good cop.

Cotton MacNeil—The not-so-good cop.

Lisa Crenshaw—The radio program manager formed the first line of defense between Bummpt and the FCC.

Prologue

The childhood shows the man,
As morning shows the day.
    —John Milton (1608-74),
      Paradise Regained

Slice the night.
Split the screen.
Slit a throat.
I could do them all with equal aplomb, equal skill.
But what I'd failed to take into account on this par-
ticular occasion was the woman. Ah yes…the woman.

I glanced at the empty page, a place I'd intended to
fill with small mementos of the case. But the page was
empty. And it was all her fault. She wasn't supposed
to be there, curled up on one side of the bed as if
trying to put as much distance as she could between
herself and the twisted mind of the man next to her.
Every night for the past week since I'd been observing
them, she'd slept on the couch, refusing to share the
marital bed.

Not that anyone would blame her.

How long had it taken for her to realize what a
sleaze her new husband was? How many nights under

his roof, under his thumb, had she survived before she crawled out of his bed and slept elsewhere? How long could she have taken that abuse and still stay sane?

Poor dear...

But I didn't allow sympathy to dissuade me from my appointed task. After all, she was an adult, fully cognizant of the devil's deal she made for herself. Sympathy for her predicament wouldn't have prevented me from ridding the world of someone who personified the evils of the night. After all, what sort of man hid in your mind night after night, turning pleasant dreams into nightmares?

The man had to be stopped.

And I was just the person to do it.

With a sigh, I closed the book, knowing the page had to remain empty, a symbol of my failure to accurately assess a situation. Then after a moment, inspiration hit.

I pulled the knife from its scabbard, pleased that the blade was still moist with tiny red dew drops. With the flick of my wrist, I wiped the remaining blood onto the page. Only a tiny smear of red marred the page, but that was enough to satisfy me. There would be no blank pages in my life. Each one would hold a memento....

This memento, this blood had belonged to that cursed creature of the night and that was indeed the most important souvenir to take from that occasion. Perhaps now the nightmares that punctuated my sleep would stop and dark clouds would cease from crowding his dreams.

Perhaps now there would be no more things that go bump in the night.

I hoped...

Chapter One

Sweat clung to Matthew's chest as he shot upright in bed. During that split second between sleep and wakefulness, he'd truly thought his nightmare had hitched a ride along with his consciousness in hopes of staining reality with the dangers that normally lurked only in his mind.

The phone rang again.

And all the terrors of the night returned from the dark recesses of his mind from whence they came.

He threw back the blanket, fumbled with the telephone receiver, and coughed, trying to clear a sleep-clogged throat. "H'llo?"

"Matt?" a weak voice asked.

His fingers tightened around the phone. He recognized the voice. He'd never forgotten that voice.

"Mattie, it hurts."

"Carol?" he whispered hoarsely. "Is that you?"

"Carol... I'm Carol Mc...McFadden, now. At least I was." There was a noise as if she'd dropped the phone.

"Carol, what's wrong? Where are you?" Adrenaline surged through him, eradicating the last shreds of exhaustion. "Carol, answer me."

There was a scraping noise, then she spoke again. "I don't like blood, Matt. You know that, more than anybody." Her voice broke and came back sounding even weaker. "And there's so much blood."

Matthew wanted to shout, but he knew what sort of adverse affect it would have on his sister, especially when she was in this state. He kept his voice low and even. "Carol, can you tell me what happened?"

The moment of silence that followed scared him more than any words would have. After an elongated pause, she spoke with a terrible sense of finality. "He's dead. At least, I think he's dead. There's so much blood." She sniffed. "Of course, I think some of it's mine...." Her voice faded away.

"Your blood?" The mental image came close to destroying his fragile control. "You have to tell me where you are, Carol. I'll send help—"

"No!" She came back strong, blurting the word, almost as a groan. But when she spoke again, her voice sounded even weaker, as if the denial had drained the last of her strength. "You come, Mattie. You're the only one I trust. The only one who understands."

"I understand, sweetheart," he crooned, his heart breaking. "I understand. Now tell me where you are."

A note of vague hysteria edged her words. "I'm in the bedroom, silly. Where else do you wake up from your nightmares?" A loud clatter made Matthew jerk the receiver from his ear for a moment—she'd dropped the telephone again. Matthew pressed the instrument closer to his ear, hoping to make out her slurred words.

"Where else would you...expect to find...things that go bump in the night? Where else do people die?"

She started to giggle but it quickly turned into a mournful wail.

"Carol? Carol!"

Her howl turned into the steady buzz of a dial tone.

FLASHING LIGHTS split the darkness of the upscale neighborhood, bouncing off suburban walls and shining through middle-class windows. If the neighbors were watching the proceedings, they were doing it from behind the anonymity of their curtains. The only people Matthew could see were the professionals whose job it was to handle this sort of mess.

Mess.

Such an anonymous word for such personal devastation.

When he reached the front of the house and encountered the policeman there, Matthew automatically reached for his wallet in order to pull out his press credentials. Then he realized that his right to be there had a basis other than a journalistic one.

"I'm...Mrs. McFadden's b-brother," he stuttered to the uniformed man who guarded the door.

The man nodded and allowed him to enter.

It wasn't difficult to find his sister. Matthew simply retraced the path of death through the house, stepping around the various clusters of forensic specialists intense in their efforts.

As he passed by the master bedroom, he shuddered, trying to ignore the splatter that marred the pastel walls of the room.

In my bedroom, silly, Carol had said.

Just beyond the bedroom door, the hallway was blocked by paramedics who hovered over Carol, frantically treating her. They barked orders and briskly repeated vital statistics. Inside the bedroom, the pace was much less frenzied; the medical examiner's team was working on a single body, taking their measurements and collecting their samples at an almost leisurely pace.

Matthew turned away from the sight and stepped as close as he dared to Carol, trying to find a balance between his need to be close to his sister yet not disturb the professionals at work.

Strangely enough, despite her obvious injuries, Carol looked very much like she did the last time their paths had crossed. Only that time she'd been throwing things at him, giving in to her temper as well as her irrational fears.

But this time, she was lying perfectly still, unaware of the Herculean efforts being made to save her life. And Matthew was the one left to face his fears, irrational or otherwise.

She was his family, his only family.

She *had* to live.

A police officer squatting near the proceedings glanced up and spotted him. "Get out of here, Childs," he said in a rough voice. "No press allowed."

"Tony…she's my sister."

The policeman initially scowled at Matthew, but a moment later, the man's anger and doubt seemed to fade away. "Jeez…I'm sorry, man. The lieutenant will want to talk to you, then."

Matthew tried not to stare at his sister's deathly white face. "I'm not leaving Carol."

"It's not as bad as it looks," one paramedic offered as he worked on her. "She's not in any real danger now. We've stopped the bleeding and her vitals are stable, now. We're just waiting for the okay to transport her.''

Thus assured, Matthew allowed himself to be conducted out of the hallway and into a study which had been untouched by any signs of crime other than that perpetrated by a vengeful decorator.

The room reeked of testosterone gone rampant. Stuffed, mounted animal heads leered from three of the four mahogany-paneled walls. Sprinkled between the animal heads were various framed magazine covers, all sporting the smirking face of the same man in various poses. The fourth wall contained a larger-than-life oil painting of a nude woman in a pose which violated several laws of decency as well as gravity.

It fully exceeded Matthew's definition of pornography.

At least he could take small consolation that it wasn't a painting of his sister.

A voice interrupted his uneasy reverie.

"If you ever listened to the bastard on the radio, then maybe it's not so surprising to see something…like this in his house.''

"I'd rather listen to silence than 'Bummpt in the Night,'" Matthew answered, before even turning around. He knew the voice; Sidney Morrison, one of the older homicide cops who had just moved into this district from downtown.

"Childs, what th' hell you doing here? I thought you'd been laid off from the paper. I gotta run you out of here, you know.''

Matthew slowly shook his head. "I wasn't laid off. I took a leave of absence.'' He tried to drag in a deep breath, but his body wasn't cooperating. "And I have every right in the world to be here. Carol McFadden is my sister." He spun around and stared straight at the man. "What happened, Sid?"

Sid shrugged. "Someone with a big temper and a bigger knife must have finally taken exception to Mr. McFadden's sparkling repartee." He waved a hand at the framed magazine covers. "Is it any wonder? Dan 'Bummpt' McFadden has alienated practically every ethnic and racial group in the country. It'd be easier to eliminate the handful of people who didn't want to kill him."

His meaning hung unspoken in the air.

"Is my sister a suspect?"

Sid shrugged. "According to the paramedic, her cuts might be considered defensive ones, the sort of injuries someone receives while fending off an attacker with a knife. But—" the man glanced back at the painting "—looks can be deceiving."

"Damn it, Sid, you don't think—"

"Sorry. Lieutenant?" A uniformed policeman appeared in the open doorway. "Meat wagon's here to move the body and the paramedics are about to transport the victim to Good Shepherd."

Morrison nodded and waved the man away. "Now you were—"

Matthew moved toward the door. "Can it, Sid. I'm going to the hospital with my sister."

The lieutenant placed a restraining hand on Matthew's arm. "Don't go. I have more questions."

Matthew stared at the thin rubber glove protecting the man's hand and his stomach surged. "Can't this wait until later? My sister needs me."

Sid almost smiled. "You're a doctor, now, too? Listen, Matt, you can do her more good by staying here and answering a few questions for me than you can pacing the waiting room and drinking stale coffee. You *do* want to catch her attacker, don't you?''

Matthew sagged against the edge of the desk and folded his arms. Carol had already lived six years without his help. Maybe she could hang on for another hour. He released a sigh. ''So…ask.''

They went through the usual questions, searching for the same data Matthew would have collected as a journalist: who, when, how, where, why. The only difference was that he had very few of the answers. After ten minutes of interrogation, Sid scratched his head with the tip of his pen. Matthew had played poker with the man enough times to know it was an unconscious sign he gave when holding a bad hand.

''So you're telling me you don't even know your own infamous brother-in-law?'' Sid added a weak smile. ''I should be so lucky…my sister married a real idiot. But on second thought, he's any anonymous idiot.''

Matthew shrugged. ''I didn't even know Carol was married.''

Sid raised an eyebrow. ''You didn't? Your own sister? Jeez, I knew every guy my sister even thought about dating. And if Mrs. McFadden had been *my* sister…'' Morrison glanced ruefully at the painting again, then turned away.

Matthew shared the man's sentiment. Dan ''Bummpt in the Night'' McFadden prided himself on his irreverent reputation as *Talk Radio's* Bad Boy, spewing his nightly dose of raunchy, prejudiced and explicitly sexual banter from coast to coast on his syndicated show.

The lewd, crude picture on the wall was vintage Bummpt material. But the rest of the house wasn't.

But it wasn't Carol's influence, either. It matched neither the style nor the taste of the sister he'd grown up with. The house was elegantly furnished with expensive pieces of objets d'art and bore the tasteful but cold impersonal stamp of a high-priced decorator. Of course, the study looked as if it has been decorated by a high-priced call girl.

"...since you talked to her?"

Matthew realized Sid was asking another question. "What? Sorry, I lost track for a moment."

"I asked how long it's been since you saw your sister or talked to her."

"Six years. We'd had some problems between us and were...estranged." Even the word sounded like *strangers* which was what they'd become—complete strangers to each other.

"Then how did you know where she lived? What address to send the police to when she called you? A bigwig celebrity like this has everything unlisted."

"Including the fact that he was married. Did you ever hear any press about Bummpt getting married?"

Sid shook his head. "No, but I don't keep up with slime like him. I get enough of the filth he vomits on the streets."

"Me, too. But you hear things now and then, especially in my trade. This whole marriage bit must have been kept under wraps. I never heard anything about it."

"That's all well and good, but it still doesn't answer my question. How did you figure out where she was when she called?"

It hit Matthew from nowhere—this sudden need to see Carol again, to be reassured that she would truly survive this ordeal. After all, she'd turned to him when she found herself in dire straits. After six years, she'd called him because she'd needed him....

And he was going to be there for her.

"We're going over the same material again, Sid. Can't we do this later? I'm the only family she has. If something goes—" the word caught in his throat "—wrong, I'm the only person who can okay any medical procedures."

Sid seemed unmoved by the plea. "If something happens, the paramedics know exactly where you are and how to get in touch with you." He tapped his pencil on his notebook. "Now, as to your relationship with your sister. Let's take it a step further back. Tell me—if you hadn't kept up with your sister in years, then how did she know where *you* lived? Considering how badly she was bleeding, she sure didn't have time to pull out a phone book and look you up."

Matthew closed his eyes. "Did you grow up living in the same house the entire time?"

"Yeah. Fifty-sixth and Grand Avenue, by the tracks. My mom lived there until she passed away a couple of years ago."

He opened his eyes. "Then you remember your old phone number, right?"

A half smile played on the policeman's lips. "Sure— Who doesn't remember things like that?"

"Exactly my point. I live in the same house that we both grew up in. Same phone number, too. Carol could have dialed that number in her sleep." His thoughts veered in an uncomfortable direction. *Or while practically bleeding to death.*

Sid nodded. "That answers the first part. What about the second? How did you know where *she* lived?"

Matthew's mind wandered back to the strained conversation. "Carol told me her last name was now McFadden. Then before she passed out, she said something about things that go bump in the night."

"So you immediately put those things together and came up with the right name? The exact address? All this ignoring the fact that this place is unlisted?"

Matthew pointed to a newspaper that sat in a nearby trash can. "Remember who I work for, Sid. What I don't have filed away up here—" he tapped his temple "—I can find out from the paper. After I called 911 and gave them Carol's number from my caller ID, it didn't take a genius to connect the name, McFadden, with 'Bummpt in the Night.' I called the paper and got his address from them. Then I came straight here."

"You ever meet this McFadden guy? Person to person?"

Matthew shook his head. "Can't say I've had the pleasure. I know him strictly by his reputation."

Sid darkened visibly. "I sure wouldn't want my sister marrying someone like him. Damn radio pervert."

Sid was fishing for motive and Matthew knew it. He wasn't afraid. "I can't say I'm happy about it...or surprised. When Carol was younger, she always had odd taste in men."

"Odd." The lieutenant coughed. "Now there's an understatement for you." He studied his notes. "You got any idea how long they've been married? Whether there was a prenup or anything like that?" His gaze narrowed. "Is your sister prone to violence?"

Matthew managed to rein in his brief flare of temper and adopt a flat tone in his response. "Like I said before, I have no idea how long they've been married.

It could have been months or it could be years. I haven't seen or spoken with Carol in six years."

The detective raised an eyebrow and almost smirked. "A lot can happen in six years."

"Excuse me, Lieutenant Morrison?" The same uniformed officer who interrupted them earlier did so again. "One of the neighbors is outside. You need to hear his story."

Sid glanced at Matt. "I guess it wouldn't work if I told you stay here and not touch anything, right? If you stay, you snoop. If you go with me, you eavesdrop." He paused for a moment. "I'd rather have you where I can see you. C'mon."

They followed the patrolman through the house and out the door. Matthew steeled himself for the sight of blood and this time made it through the gauntlet of crime without undue stress.

They approached another officer and his companion, a bathrobed man in his early sixties. The strands of hair that he usually combed over his bald spot were hanging down the side of his head, almost touching his shoulder.

"Mr. Parker lives next door." The uniformed officer turned toward the man. "Why don't you tell the lieutenant what you told me, sir?"

The left corner of Parker's lip curled in an unattractive sneer. "That McFadden guy? He's a real pain. He's all the time crabbing about something—the leaves, my dog, the fence between our property. Just between you and me? If someone offed him, then they probably did it to shut him up. Jeez, I've never met a guy who loved the sound of his own voice more than McFadden."

"What about his wife? You know her?"

Parker shrugged. "She's quiet, seems nice, a little mousy. Nothing like her husband, but hey? Who could get a word in edgewise with a blowhard like that?"

"Did they seem happy?"

Parker's bushy eyebrows drew together. "How th' hell would I know? You think I'm some Peeping Tom who hangs by their bedroom window watching and trying to eavesdrop on his neighbors?"

Sid backpedaled quickly. "That's not what I mean at all, sir. It's just that you know how arguments can sometimes spill out into the open air and—"

"Yeah, yeah, I know what you mean." Parker dismissed the thought with a wave of his hand. "I have no idea if they were happy or what. All I know was that he was a real pain. And that kid of theirs—"

Matthew felt his heart wedge itself into his throat.

A child?

SHE WOKE WITH A START, adrenaline exploding through her veins, making her heart pump and her breath come in short gasps. Her son's plaintive cry penetrated the world beyond her dreams and echoed in her ears.

Her first instinct was to run to his room, to soothe away his fears and find Mr. Popster, his stalwart companion. Then she remembered.

He wasn't there.

Something inside of her twisted.

His bed would be empty.

She struggled to control her runaway heart.

His bed would be empty for several more nights.

She drew in a strangled gasp of air.

But he'll be back. She closed her eyes, forcing herself to lie down again. *He'll be back soon....*

Somewhere in the dark she heard him cry again. And this time, she joined in.

Chapter Two

Despite Sid's suggestion to stay clear, Matthew knew he had to join the search. Too many things could have happened in the six years since he'd last seen his sister. One of which could have been the birth of a child.

The concept of *I might be an uncle…* wasn't nearly as frightening as the idea *Carol might be a mother.* Carol simply wasn't mother material. At least, not the last time he saw her. She was still trying to live her life like a college kid, boozing it up all night and trying to keep up some semblance of normalcy during the day. She'd possessed neither the sense of maternity nor maturity to be responsible for an innocent little life.

After following the lieutenant into the green bedroom, Matthew closed his eyes, trying to concentrate.

A child.

Scared. Hiding.

Where was he hiding?

A bright light flared in Matthew's head. *Where would I have hidden?* The light grew harsher. *Where did I hide?*

He reached out and tapped the policeman on the shoulder. "Sid, the kid's in his own room," he whispered, unable to speak any louder. "That's where he'd go. That's where he'd feel safe."

The lieutenant shot him a scowl. "I got kids. You don't. What suddenly makes you the expert on kids?"

Matthew felt the blood drain from his face. "I've been there. Before."

Sid stared at him a moment, then he lifted one shoulder in resignation. "Okay, supposing you're right, have you seen anything around here that even looks remotely like a little kid's room?"

Matthew opened his mouth, then closed it without speaking. Sid was right. The bedrooms all bore the same sterile stamp of an unenthusiastic decorator, all designed for adults. There was no room which contained what you'd expect in a child's room. Matthew remembered his own room, crammed full of toys, books and those gawd-awful cartoon character curtains his aunt had made for him.

"C'mon." Sid led the way and together they began to search.

Each bedroom had been color-coordinated to within an inch of its life. The blue room, the green room, the yellow room. Matthew winced—a decorator with only a pallet of primary colors. Not a single bedroom looked as if it could have belonged to a child—whole, half or step.

More importantly, none of the beds had been slept in other than the one in the master bedroom where Bummpt's body had been discovered. Matthew refused to consider the idea that the child could have been in bed with his parents when the attacker struck. The mental picture was more than he was willing to tolerate.

However, logic argued, motherhood would certainly

explain Carol's defensive cuts. *A mother protecting her young....*

Matthew turned to suggest the idea to Sid, but the man had already abandoned his search of the green bedroom.

For greener pastures?

As Matthew exited, he suddenly caught sight of something above the door. Stopping, he craned his neck for a better look. Perched on the top of the wooden door frame sat a single green plastic soldier, just like the type he'd played with as a kid. The green ivy wallpaper print had provided an apt jungle to camouflage the toy sitting above the doorway.

He pivoted slowly, suddenly sensing he wasn't alone in the room. His first instinct was to yell for Sid, but he realized that if there was indeed a child in the room, that would frighten him or her even more. Yet Matthew couldn't bring himself to leave the bedroom.

Something was making him stay. Something or someone.

"It's safe," he whispered. "You can come out, now."

He heard nothing other than the sounds of the police talking in lowered voices as they searched the rest of the house.

Matthew addressed the middle of the room. "The bad guy's gone and there's no one but the police around now. They're not going to hurt you. They're here to protect you."

Silence?

Or… Was it his imagination or had he heard a small sniffle?

There was only one way to find out.

He addressed the bed. "It must have been really

scary for you. I sure know I would've been scared. I would have hidden, too. That was awfully smart of you.''

Sniff.

There.

He'd definitely heard something, a sniffle.

There was a kid in the room. Somewhere. But where? Matthew moved closer to the bed and knelt down. He lifted the dust ruffle carefully. ''My name is Matt.''

There was nothing under the bed. Not even a ball of dust. Carol's decorator might have been lazy, but her maid was evidently overzealous.

Matthew moved toward a large overstuffed chair which sat in a corner of the room by a window. He shifted the curtain out of the way to look behind the chair.

''But listen,'' he continued, ''I'm not a policeman. So if you'd rather see one all dressed up in his uniform with a badge and everything so you can be sure it's really a policeman, you tell me and I'll go get one, okay?'' Maybe a conversational tone might draw the child out, break through his defenses, even trick him into speaking.

But there was no response. Not even the telltale sniff.

Matthew turned around and scanned the room for other likely hiding places. The closet? But they'd checked there, once before. Yet something inside told Matthew they hadn't been thorough enough.

He crossed the room, reached out for the doorknob, then paused. ''Did you ever hear—'' he almost said *your mom,* but couldn't bring himself to say those words ''—Carol talk about her brother? Matthew?

That's me. So, I guess I'm your Uncle Matt. Carol and I grew up together on the other side of town. Did she ever tell you about our dog, Carlotta? She was a German shepherd who had been a police dog. Carlotta knew how to play hide-and-seek better than any dog I ever knew.''

There was a discernible sniff from somewhere near the closet.

''Really?'' a small voice asked.

Matthew's heart began to race. He glanced toward the hallway and saw a passing patrolman whom he flagged down with a silent wave.

The man stepped into the room and began to speak. ''Si—''

Matthew cut him off with a curt gesture, pointed at the closet, then outside. ''Get Lieutenant Morrison,'' he mouthed. The uniformed man stared for a moment, then his face brightened and he rushed out of sight.

Matthew turned back to the problem at hand. ''Really and truly,'' he declared in the most positive voice he could conjure. ''But I have to admit something.'' He lowered his voice into a conspiratorial whisper. ''I haven't played hide-and-seek since I grew up so I'm a little rusty at it. As far as that goes, I've never been an uncle before so you'd sorta have to help me with lots of things. Okay?''

''O-okay.''

The pain in the small voice almost broke Matthew's heart. No child should suffer through something like this alone. Someone needed to help him. And if it was going to become Matthew's responsibility, then so be it. He adopted his best nonconfrontational tone. ''So, is it all right for me to open the closet door and say 'Olly olly oxen free?''

"Okay." There was a moment of silence. "But I'm not in the closet."

The flowered tablecloth which covered the small bedside table shifted slightly. A corner lifted and Matthew had the sudden, distinct feeling he was being scrutinized to see if he met muster as uncle material. He waved at the small semicircle of darkness beneath the tablecloth's bottom edge, knowing it hid a child's scrutinizing stare.

"Hi." He added the best smile he could generate, considering the circumstances

"Hi. You're it."

The tiny voice was so soft, so sweet that Matthew began to think he might have a niece rather than a nephew. His smile broadened into something more genuine on its own. "Not, I'm not Cousin Itt. I'm Uncle Matt."

The child sniffed. "I'm Danny."

A boy. Obviously named after his father, Daniel. Had that been Carol's idea or her husband's?

"You want to come on out from beneath there? It's a pretty good hiding place."

Danny said nothing.

"Danny, it's safe. I promise."

A childish sigh echoed through the room. "Is the bogeyman gone?"

Matthew echoed his sigh. "Yeah, the bogeyman is long gone. It's safe, now."

The tablecloth rustled and suddenly, the child bolted from his hiding place, launching himself sobbing into Matthew's arms. Locking his plaid-flannel-clad legs around Matthew's waist, Danny also latched on to Matthew's neck, nearly cutting off his oxygen supply. Unable and unwilling to break the child's death grip on perceived safety, Matthew backed up until they ended up sitting in the chair in the corner of the room.

He murmured soothing things in the child's ear, the same sort of words that had comforted him so many years ago. They started rocking, falling easily into that ageless rhythm that one used when trying to console the distraught and create harmony out of total discord.

As the child wept into his shirt, Matthew found himself promising all sorts of things, all of which he intended to keep, especially his most important promise: *"I won't let anybody hurt you."*

No matter if this was Carol's son or her stepson, Matthew knew that he had to do all that was within his power to keep this child from any further harm. The thought was so overpowering that when Sid stepped back into the room, Matthew instinctively tightened his grip on the child.

"Good job, Childs. Looks like you were right, after all."

Danny jumped, despite the fact that Sid spoke in a very quiet voice. Matthew turned his reflexive grasp into a hug, then loosened it purposefully. The lieutenant had children; he knew enough not to rush the situation.

"Danny, this is Mr. Morrison. He's a friend of mine." Matthew planted a kiss on the top of the child's fine hair. The oddly reassuring smell of Ivory soap and baby shampoo tickled his nose. "Sid, this is my...nephew, Danny."

Danny turned his head slightly so he could take a furtive glance at Sid. "He's a f-friend?"

Matthew nodded resolutely. "Definitely a friend. In fact, he was the good guy who got here first because he wanted to help you. All I did was find you. Sid, here—'' he nodded toward the man ''—was the one who chased away the bad guys.''

''Bad guy,'' Danny corrected. ''The bogeyman.''

Matt and Sid shared an important look. How much had Danny seen? And more importantly, how much did the killer think he'd seen?

''You sure there was only one?'' Sid asked.

Danny imitated Matthew's resolute nod. ''Everyone knows there's only one bogeyman.''

Sid released the breath he held. He ruffled the child's hair. ''You got that right, kiddo. I'll catch him and I'll book 'em, Dano.''

Once they got out of the house, Danny finally released the choke hold on his new uncle's neck. But Matthew's hand was a whole other story. Danny held it as if letting go meant becoming lost in the wilderness forever.

When asked his age, Danny held up three fingers, furrowed his brow, then held up a fourth one. He volunteered little else about himself, but seemed agreeable as well as truthful when it came to answering questions.

Sid squatted down, trying to approach the child, eye to eye. ''What's your mommy's name?''

''Mommy,'' Danny answered solemnly.

Sid glanced at Matthew.

Ask a silly question.

Sid tried again. ''What's your daddy's name?''

''Daddy. But some people call him 'Bummpt.'''

Sid's look said, *Now we're getting somewhere.*

''He talks on the radio, right?''

Danny nodded. ''Uh-huh.''

''What does your mommy do?''

Danny shrugged. "Mommy things. Office things, too."

Sid offered the child a smile. "Do you know the telephone number for your mommy's office?"

Danny screwed his face up in deep thought. After a moment, he shook his head. "No." He brightened suddenly. "But I do know my telephone number! It's 555-6123. And I'm four!"

Matthew's stomach clenched, but he squeezed the child's hand, not wanting to telegraph his sudden influx of feelings. "Very good, Danny. You sure are a smart kid."

Sid stood up, brushing off the knees of his pants. "Definitely Harvard material, give or take fifteen years."

Danny wrapped his arms around Matthew's leg, seemingly content to cling there. Matthew leaned closer to the policeman, trying to keep his heart from plunging to the pits of his stomach. "He just answered a very important question, too."

Sid raised an eyebrow. "That Mommy works in an office?"

Matthew shook his head. "That Carol's not his mother. 555-6123 isn't the McFadden's telephone number. I don't think that's even a local exchange." Matthew reached down and swung Danny up into his arms. "Hey sport, tell me about your Aunt Carol."

Danny shrugged and toyed with a button on Matthew's shirt. "She's okay."

"Just okay?"

Danny sighed in a manner that far surpassed his tender years. "She doesn't know much about kids. No 'sperience. Momma says Aunt Carol means well, but she's got no 'sperience."

Matthew nodded, bowing to the child's uncanny wisdom. It looked as if Carol hadn't changed much in the past six years; she always meant well, but her execution— Matthew stopped himself, knowing that he didn't want to use the word *execution* in any context. He tried to smile at his "nephew."

"So is your mommy staying at home this weekend while you're here visiting your daddy?"

Danny shrugged again. "Guess so." He yawned and nuzzled Matthew's shoulder as if trying to find a comfortable spot.

Sid patted the child's back and after only a few seconds of reassuring rhythm, Danny's heavy eyelids began to close.

Sid sighed. "Kids. They can fall asleep anywhere, anytime. During a hurricane, an earthquake—"

"—after a murder?"

Sid made a face. "Guess I need to call social services and get him in temporary care tonight until we find his mother."

Matthew automatically tightened his hold on the child. "Sid, don't do it. He seems perfectly willing to accept me as his Uncle Matt. Let me take him to my place until his mom gets here."

Sid planted his fists on his hips. "One little problem—you're not his Uncle Matt."

Matthew shifted his sleepy load to a better position. "Sure I am. My sister is his Aunt Carol. That makes me his Uncle Matt…at least for tonight. You can vouch to the various authorities as well as his mother that I'm an upstanding, moral citizen and that I'll take good care of him until she gets here. Anyway, this is no place for a kid. Especially at this age."

"Well…" Sid glanced around at the activity which

still bustled in and around the house, then his gaze settled on the child's peaceful face. "Makes sense, I guess. You two head on home, then. I'll call you with an update."

Matthew shifted his load once more, in order to reach into his pocket and get his car keys. Danny roused, rubbing his eyes. "I want my mommy."

"Shh, go back to sleep. Mr. Morrison is calling your mom and she'll pick you up at my house, okay?"

Danny's face began to pucker. "I want my mommy, now." He began to cry. "Mom-mee..."

Sid reached up and patted Danny's back. "Listen, kiddo, you'll be safe with your Uncle Matt and just as soon as your momma gets here, I'll bring her right to you, okay? I'm a policeman, you know, so I can drive her really fast in my squad car with the sirens on and the lights flashing."

This seemed to pique Danny's interest. "A real siren?"

Sid nodded. "And flashing lights. Red ones *and* blue ones, too."

Danny wiped his eyes as well as his nose on the shoulder of Matthew's shirt. "Okay," the boy said, begrudgingly. His face puckered once more. "But I can't sleep without Mr. Popster."

Matthew and Sid exchanged grimaces.

Sid managed the first smile. "And Mr. Popster is...?"

"Mr. Popster," Danny said, as if that was explanation enough.

Five minutes later, a patrolman brought out a bedraggled stuffed toy that Danny had left under the bedside hiding place. Danny buried his face in the material which has once been white, then released a sigh of undisguised relief. The patrolman who delivered the toy smiled knowingly then started to leave. He stopped, pivoted and reached into his pocket and pulled out a green plastic army man.

"I found this over the door in that room. Since it was the only other toy in the place, I thought the kid might like to have it with him, too."

Danny wrapped his fingers around the plastic figure and pulled it to his chest beside Mr. Popster.

"What do you say?" Matthew prompted, feeling a sudden surge of paternity.

Danny buried his face, evidently having been hit with a sudden case of shyness. "Thank you," he muttered.

Sid clapped Matthew on the shoulder. "Watch out. If the women around here see this natural fatherhood pouring from you, you'll be the next head on the matrimonial block."

Matthew felt his guts twist; not at the prospect of marriage, but at Sid's particular brand of gallows humor. McFadden had practically been decapitated by a knife and it seemed unconscionable to speak quite so lightly about sacrificing one's head to any cause.

Sid ruffled the child's hair. "You take care of your Uncle Matt, okay, Danny?"

"Uh-huh." The child yawned and closed his eyes, his fist still clenched on his army man.

"Bogeyman won't get me," he whispered quietly.

"Bogeyman won't get me...."

"Bogeyman won't..."

Danny fell asleep.

DANNY STAYED ASLEEP during the entire trip home until Matthew carried him into the guest room. As soon as the child's head touched the pillow, his eyes sprang open and his arms shot out.

"No!" He placed a stranglehold on Matthew's neck. "Don't leave me."

No amount of consolation would ease the child. He refused to stay in a strange bedroom alone, not that Matthew could blame him. Bedrooms had bad connotations at the moment. The only place where the child seemed the least bit at ease was the living room, curled up with a pillow, a blanket and his two toys in an old recliner that Matthew had found during his scavenging college days.

Although only a child, Danny had instinctively chosen a place where his chair backed into a corner of the room. From that vantage point, he could see every window and door that led into the room, meaning no one could sneak up behind him.

Matthew knew those protective instincts quite well. He tucked the blanket around Danny, only to have his careful work disturbed by the child who insisted that his army man be placed on guard duty on the chair's arm.

"I'm going to make some coffee. I'll be in the kitchen and—"

"No! Don't leave."

Matthew smiled. "I'm not leaving, sport. I'm just going into the kitchen." He stared at the little face which began to pucker. "Okay, okay. What if I keep talking while I'm in there? You can hear me in here and you'll know everything's all right. Okay?"

"Okay."

Matthew headed for the kitchen. "So, tell me a little about yourself, Danny. Do you go to school?"

"Uh-huh. Preschool."

Matthew filled the empty pot from the faucet and dumped it into the back of the coffee maker. "What's your teacher's name?"

"Mrs. R. We call her that 'cause her name's so hard to 'nounce."

"That makes sense. I had a teacher named Mrs. Benstermacher and I wish we could have called her Mrs. B. So...do you like school?"

"Uh-huh."

"What's your favorite subject?" It was a toss-up: either recess or lunch. The answer surprised him.

"Art. I like to draw."

"Really? That's neat. I'm not very good at drawing. I wish I was. What do you like to draw? I bet it's army men, right?"

"Nope. Omega Rangers."

Another surprising answer. As attached as Danny was to the figurine, Matthew thought it might signify a more involved level of interest.

"So, you got a best friend in your class?"

"Yeah. Justin." This time the answer sounded definitely sleepy.

Matthew stared at the empty pot, waiting for the sputtering stream of coffee to begin. He started talking about school, saying anything he could think of to fill the silence that Danny feared. By the time he'd filled his cup, he'd run out of school-oriented anecdotes.

He came into the living room, tentatively sipping the coffee. "Tell me about your mom—"

Danny had fallen asleep, but it wasn't a restful one. Evidently bad dreams were already invading his slumber. The child squirmed in his sleep, knocking his plastic guardian to the floor. Matthew retrieved the toy and tucked it in the sleeping child's hand. As if by magic, Danny calmed down, his nightmares abating.

Matthew sat on the floor next to the chair, leaning against the footrest.

Imagine, being four years old and having to face this sort of horror in your life.

Matthew drew in a mouthful of scalding coffee, welcoming the pain which helped chase away his own demons. He'd thought it had been bad enough, facing the same sort of thing when he was six.

At six, you understood things that a four-year-old couldn't. At six, bogeymen didn't invade your dreams; real people did. And everybody knew that truth was stranger, and deadlier, than fiction.

He blew into his coffee mug, feeling the steam leave a damp sheen across his face.

It was going to be a long night.

Chapter Three

Jillian Kincaid's knuckles whitened as she twisted the steering wheel with more savagery than usual. The car bumped over the curb of the driveway and lurched to a jarring stop. As the engine died, so did the last vestiges of her strength. She closed her eyes and sent up a hasty prayer.

Please...please let Danny be all right.

The call she'd received had been remarkably uninformative. Her ex-husband was dead and her son had been present in the house when it occurred.

Her first reaction?

It had to be a heart attack. Rampant hedonism must have taken its toll on Daniel "Bummpt" McFadden. Bummpt drank, smoked and did everything to excess, but not merely for the sake of his radio image, as she first thought.

What she'd thought was a facade—the foul language, the constant barrage of sexual innuendoes, the joy of constantly stirring the proverbial hornets' nest—was his real personality. The kind, gentle man who insisted his radio persona was all a gimmick, that in reality Daniel McFadden was a quiet conservative man, an actor of sorts, that had been the man she thought she loved.

But the facade soon wore away to reveal the frighteningly real man beneath.

Daniel ''Bummpt in the Night'' McFadden was truly the stuff that nightmares were made of.

But then the person who called her, reporting his death, dealt another card.

Murder.

It had been one thing to worry about Danny's well-being in light of what she perceived as his father's possible heart attack. But something else completely different to learn that her son had been living, albeit temporarily, in the same house where his father had just been murdered.

The image it conjured in the mind's eye was of Danny, standing in bloodied pajamas and clutching his beloved Mr. Popster. The very thought of it had made her sink to her knees in panic. But the police hastened to assure her they believed Danny had not seen anything during or after what they called ''the attack.'' But no matter what they said, it remained her duty to determine what Danny had and hadn't seen and deal with it, as quickly as possible.

And thanks to her highway patrol escort, she'd made the usual four-hour drive between Lexington and Middletown in record time, the bloody spectral image of her ex-husband haunting every white-knuckled mile of the distance.

It wasn't until after she'd been passed off to the local police and the patrolman had signaled that they'd reach their destination that she allowed herself to acknowledge the strength of the emotions that waged a bid for her control.

Fear.

Anger.

Helplessness.

Unacceptable images of death and dying and a very small, frightened child flashed behind her eyes. When she opened them, she realized tears blurred her vision, preventing her from focusing on the seat belt mechanism. Wiping her sleeve across her face, she allowed herself a rare expletive. Cursing was a habit she'd forced herself to break the day she discovered she was pregnant.

There were lots of things she'd given up when motherhood blossomed.

Cigarettes. Booze. Caffeine.

And strangely enough, out of three of them, the one she craved the most at that very moment was the caffeine. A good sign, she guessed. She managed to unstrap herself from the seat and open the door. A blast of cold air hit her, making her jump.

Caffeine. Yeah, as if I need something to make me even more jumpy.

"Ma'am?"

She flinched, then forced herself to look up into the face of the patrolman whose car she'd followed. He offered her a polite smile and a helping hand. She'd never had much use for cops before, in an earlier life. To have them be so solicitous and courteous now was almost unsettling.

Yet, she appreciated his calm strength, even if it was born of his emotional distance from the very facts that made her stomach twist and her mind reel. "Th-thanks," she said between chattering teeth as he helped extract her from the car.

He dipped his head with a deferential nod. "Yes'm.

The lieutenant said that the boy is fine…and for you not to worry.''

Easier said than done. She couldn't, she *wouldn't* believe her son was all right until she saw him with her own eyes and held him in her own arms. That very thought infused her with new energy, speeding her up the long brick stairs which led to the front door of a nice normal suburban house. Nothing like the color-coded monstrosity that Dan lived in. She'd been inside once and that was one time too many.

"Hey slow down, ma'am. You'll fall." In a considerate move, the policeman shined the bright beam of his flashlight at the stairs.

Jill continued toward the front of the house, taking the steps two at a time, expelling her breath in frosty clouds. The night was unseasonably cool, but she appreciated the bite in the air. It helped her stay alert.

A few moments later, they stood at the front door. She lifted her arm to pound on the door, to demand entrance, but her efforts to knock faltered into a barely discernible tap. The policeman reached around her and used the butt of his flashlight to rap on the door.

They heard a faint, "Come in," which was all the invitation Jill needed. She pushed the door, dismayed to find it unlocked. The police had turned her son over to some man who couldn't even be responsible enough to keep his doors locked at night? She stumbled into a dark foyer.

The voice called out, a little stronger. "In here."

She followed the sound to a living room where in the shadows, she saw a figure sitting in a large chair. As she approached, she realized he held the limp body of her son.

A scream rose in her throat, but before she could release it, the man shook his head.

"Don't panic. He's sleeping, that's all." He looked down at Danny and a strained but honest smile crossed his face. "It's been a rough night for the little guy. Bad dreams. He made me promise not to leave him." As if to demonstrate his point, Danny shifted, burrowing in the man's arms and releasing a noise which sounded suspiciously like a contented sigh.

She crossed the room in a flash, falling to her knees beside the chair. "Danny?" she whispered.

"Don't wake him," the man cautioned.

Jill allowed her sense of panic to override her better judgment. She reached for him. "He's my son!"

The man tightened his hold on Danny for a brief moment, then drew in a deep breath. "Of course. But let's find a better place…" He looked around. "Why don't you sit on the couch and let me put him in your arms? That way he might stay asleep."

It made sense. In the midst of all her fear and dread and terror, she could make herself listen to reason, couldn't she? Perhaps that should be a reassuring thought, but in reality, all she wanted was her son and she'd do anything to get him.

Now.

She drew a deep breath. "All right…" She dropped to the couch, sitting as close to the chair as possible. The man stood with surprising grace, lifting Danny with ease. A moment later, her son was in her arms.

All was right in the world.

Danny settled in quickly, his head finding its usual resting place against her shoulder. He nuzzled her and sighed, blissfully unaware of her tears which were leaving small damp circles in his silky dark hair.

At four, he was still a baby, her baby. And oh how he hated being called her baby. One time he'd explained exactly what attributes signified the end of his babyhood; he went to school, he drank chocolate milk, he'd outgrown a car seat and used only a booster seat when they rode in the car. By these reasons alone, he proclaimed that he was no longer a baby.

So there.

She kissed his head. Silly little boy. He would always be her baby. No matter how tall, no matter how old. No matter if he got as tall as his father...

Her stomach seized.

A random memory made a chill spread across the back of her neck. Her ex-husband was dead. How close had Danny been to danger? The details she'd received over the phone were sketchy at best. She'd been assured that her son hadn't witnessed the violence that took his father's life, but who could be positive? Even if he hadn't seen anything, wasn't merely being in the same house at the same time bad enough?

She glanced up at the man who towered over her, intending to ask him about Bummpt's death, but the words clogged in her throat.

Bummpt.

She'd long ago stopped thinking of him as Daniel McFadden. His syndicated radio persona had taken control years ago, doing anything, saying anything that would result in more stations, bigger markets and bigger ratings. The emotional temperature of their brief marriage had relied solely on the numbers gleaned from The Book—the quarterly Armitron ratings. A bad book meant Bummpt on a drunken rampage; a good book meant Bummpt celebrating with an endless party and a bottomless bottle.

Either way, it meant he got ripsnorting drunk and in his world, he wasn't accountable for what happened when he was drunk. That was how Danny was conceived and why she stuck around for as long as she dared.

Then she'd gotten out for her sanity and safety's sake.

Jill stared into the stranger's kind eyes, instinctively knowing that her son had been safe those few hours in his care. "Th-thank you," she managed to whisper. "Th-thank you, Mr...."

"Childs, Matthew Childs." He paused for a moment. "I'm Carol's brother." He failed to completely hide the flash of emotion that crossed his face.

Carol? Then she remembered. Bummpt's trophy wife. Blond, leggy and terribly naive. She had no direct animosity toward the woman; Carol hadn't been the one to break up their marriage. That had been another blond, leggy, naive woman who had been lulled by Bummpt's practiced patter.

Jill tried to adopt a sympathetic expression. "I'm sorry about your sister, Mr. Childs. They told me she'd been...injured. Have there been any changes?"

He shook his head. "Nothing yet. They said they'd call."

She tried to shift Danny's dead weight higher in her arms so she could eventually stand. "I suspect you want to go to the hospital and be with her." She worked her way to the edge of the couch in preparation to rise. "So I'll just take Danny and we'll head home—"

"Ms. Kincaid?"

She turned to the patrolman who had been standing there patiently in the foyer. He gestured to his walkie-talkie. "The lieutenant would rather you not leave the area for a day or two. In the morning they'd like to ask your son some questions about what he might have seen."

She shook her head. "He's only four. Even if he saw something, I doubt he could tell us anything really useful."

The patrolman shrugged. "They won't know until they talk to him." He gestured to the front door. "I'd be glad to escort you to a nearby hotel where you can check in and—"

An ear-piercing shriek halted his offer. Danny began to thrash about, obviously caught in the throes of a nightmare. Jill held on for dear life, afraid that her son would lunge out of her arms and hit the floor.

"Danny, wake up," she pleaded, trying to dodge his flailing fists. "It's Mommy. Wake up, honey. It's all right. I'm here."

Matthew reached down, plucked something from the floor and pressed it in Danny's palm. "Here, buddy. Your army man. He'll protect you, remember?"

Danny's screams faded to silence as he roused long enough to examine the toy. He clutched it to his chest and fell back asleep.

Somewhere deep inside, Jill was upset that her son hadn't even noticed her presence or taken any comfort from it. Logic told her it was because he hadn't woken up enough to realize she'd arrived, or better yet, he naturally accepted her presence as commonplace because she'd always been there to chase away the nightmares.

However, it was evident he'd been cognizant of Matthew Childs' warm, soothing voice, and also aware of the comfort of a toy—not Mr. Popster but something possessing similarly reassuring attributes.

"What did you give him?" she whispered, trying to see the object her son gripped in a tight fist.

Matthew patted Danny's back. "His army man. I think he feels better knowing someone is on alert, guarding him."

"That's a mother's job." She closed her eyes, willing her heart not to break. A job she'd evidently failed to carry out.

Uncomfortable silence filled the room.

"And a father's job, too," Matthew said in a strained voice. He cleared his throat. "Look, it's pretty evident Danny feels comfortable here. If you uproot him to some strange hotel, he's likely to get upset again, and then neither of you will get any rest." He paused. "I know it's been a hard night for him and I bet just as bad for you."

She opened her eyes and their gazes met. Compassion and concern shone plainly in his face. Up to that point, she'd been dubious of the whole situation; the police had turned her son's welfare over to a complete stranger while waiting for her to arrive. But there was something in his face, in his eyes that made her trust him, or at least want to trust him.

"I know you don't know me," he continued, "but stay here. I have plenty of room." When he glanced at Danny, a small smile tugged at his lips. "And I have a feeling Danny trusts me."

She started to speak, but he cut her off.

"Please. Stay here tonight. At least what there is left of it." He glanced at his watch "It's almost four in the morning."

Danny stirred in her arms, yawning and rousing enough to lift his head. "Momma?"

She leaned down, so her cheek touched his. "Shh…honey, Momma's here."

Danny nodded, pulled his clenched fist to his chest and released a contented sigh. "Uncle Matt says the bogeyman won't look here for me."

She forced herself not to glance up at the man standing next to them. "*Uncle* Matt says so?"

Danny murmured a sleepy "Uh-huh…"

"Well," she whispered, "if Uncle Matt says so, then it must be true." After a moment's hesitation, she turned to Matthew. "Thank you. We'd like to stay."

A SCRAPBOOK. Such a lovely set of memories contained inside. I'm not sure when I got the idea, but it became quite a game to find the right souvenir in the midst of more important duties.

Taking her ID bracelet was inspired. Unique, even. And even better, no one had missed. it. Who was going to check the hospital bracelet to make sure they were looking at one of the most popular faces in America? He'd watched her movies when he was young, identifying with the vitality she infused in her roles. But the roles changed and she stopped being innocent, simple and sweet. In the last eight years, she'd played an unending string of harsh women, bitter, complicated…hateful.

She really tore it with that damned cartoon. Cartoons were supposed to be fairy tales with fantasy characters, unbelievable plots and obligatory happy endings. But she infused herself into her character, giving a third dimension to what should have amounted to a stick figure. She gave life and breath to an otherwise flat, lifeless drawing.

And for that reason, she had to die.

The Evil Queen was a despicable woman. She terrorized the young without mercy. I saw it with my own eyes as I sat in the theater and watched the children cower in their mothers' laps. He was scared, too, but there was no convenient lap for him to hide in. And that made me angry.

How dare she cause him such fear? How dare she do it to any of the children? How dare she do it for the sake of entertainment?

I was ready to hunt her down and eradicate her when two magic words flashed on the screen.

"The End."

Suddenly the fear ended. The children were laughing and clapping, as if they didn't remember being frightened and intimidated only moments earlier by the wicked figure on the screen.

How simply, how easily those two words made everything change.

The End.

I sat there, relieved, thankful that the terror was over, that his worst fears had been abated. And then the strangest and most horrible thing imaginable happened....

The movie started over again.

That's when I knew I had to take action, to end the cycle. I had to write a new ending to this story, one that assured the world that when the words The End *flashed on the screen, it was indeed the end of life for the Evil Queen.*

I did it for him. To keep him safe and sound and allow him to enjoy his childhood in relative safety.

It was my job.

And I loved doing it.

Chapter Four

Although Matthew had offered them his guest room, Danny fought every time his mother tried to carry him out of the den. Matthew made one attempt to take him from his mother's arms, but as the screams escalated, they realized they had few options. Rather than upset Danny any more, Jill relented and the two of them ended up on the couch where she assured Matthew she'd be comfortable enough, considering the circumstances.

Once Matthew got his two guests settled with pillows and blankets, he trudged off to his own room, suddenly overwhelmed by the fatigue of interrupted sleep and the void left behind after running on pure adrenaline for a couple of hours.

He usually slept in the raw, but as a concession to decorum and his houseguests, he stripped off his clothes, ducked under a brief shower and pulled on a pair of sweats. Stretching out across his bed, Matthew closed his eyes and commanded himself to sleep. But nothing worked.

He tried every trick he knew to fall asleep, even at one point considering a stiff shot of whiskey to deaden his nerves. But this was no time for a drink. Although there was a patrolman on watch outside, Matthew had a responsibility to his guest.

Guests.

As far as rampaging mothers went, Jillian Kincaid was a total surprise. He'd expected either hysteria or the mother lion, clawing anything that stood between her and her child. But what he saw was a harried mother, who, even in the height of emotion, worked from a logical basis.

Lucky kid.

Matthew's own mother had tended to react first and think later, which made it hard on him and his sister. When his father was murdered, Matthew needed someone to trust, someone to confide in, someone to listen to him. But his mother's violently hysterical reactions to her husband's death meant the professionals concentrated on her as both chief witness and potential suspect. Matthew and Carol became secondary in importance, lost in the system and left to cope with their father's death and their mother's hysteria in whatever manner they could manage on their own. Two weeks had gone by before anyone thought to ask six-year-old Matthew what he had seen…which meant Matthew had to live a lonely nightmare for almost fourteen days, waiting for his father's killer to come back and eliminate the only eyewitness: him. Then, after finally having a chance to share the horror of it with the authorities, he suffered the greatest and scariest indignity of all; his story was discounted because of his age.

And because of that, a murderer went free.

And Matthew lived in fear. For years.

It won't happen twice.

If Danny had seen anything, Matthew was determined to make sure the child had a chance to tell the authorities and to make sure they listened. No one would discount Danny's story because of his age. No one would pat him on the head and tell him there was nothing to worry about.

No one would tell him he's silly.

No one would ignore him as he huddled in a corner, frightened for his very life.

If Matthew had any control or influence, there would be one less child forced to face his fears by himself.

Matthew punched his pillow with unusual savagery and willed himself to fall asleep.

Five minutes stretched into ten and ten into fifteen. But no matter how hard he tried to think of something, anything else, every time he closed his eyes he kept seeing Carol's white, expressionless face, marred by a single trickle of blood.

His only recourse would be to purge the image from his system in the only way he knew how—by replacing it with another, equally strong, equally horrifying, but an image he could eventually conquer.

A tragedy that had run its course.

He rose from his bed and slipped quietly through the house, pausing in the den to give his sleeping guests a quick glance. Danny looked as if he'd managed to slip the surly bonds of reality and lose himself in some fairly pleasant dreams. But his mother wasn't as lucky; even in her sleep, Jill Kincaid fiercely gripped her son as if she feared someone might try to take him away. Matthew couldn't fault her sense of intensity. In fact, he appreciated it more than she would ever know.

For a moment, he wanted to stay there, to watch them as they slept. But he felt more like a voyeur than a guardian in the night. Jill didn't look like a mother. It wasn't because she didn't possess the right sensitivities. All anyone had to do was look at her to realize she loved her son. But she didn't fill Matthew's expectations of a mother. She was too pretty, too young, too...

Competent?

Freud would have a field day with that one.

He moved soundlessly into the relative safety of his office where he could face his demons alone. There, he hunched over his computer, ready to slay with syllables and conquer with conjunctions.

He stayed there for hours.

Past dawn.

Past the time when other people where getting up on a lazy Sunday morning to read the paper over a leisurely cup of coffee.

He sweated out the words, almost aghast at how they rolled right out of his fingers, across the keyboard and onto the monitor screen. He should be guilty, he told himself. How callous was he to let the terrors of one child inspire him to write about another scared child? How dare he feed off of the fears of an innocent to fuel his own seemingly unending need to cleanse an unremovable stain?

But somehow, Danny and his fears were giving Matthew a new perspective, a stronger platform from which to look at an old story with a new slant. Matthew knew too well that a writer couldn't argue with the whys of inspiration, but merely had to obey the dictates of his own muse and write the words that came to mind.

He was deep in the midst of a painful scene that had haunted him for the better part of his life, a scene which had refused to be put in words until now. It wasn't Matthew's job to explain how the light of another tragedy could illuminate a dark past as well as it did. It was a helluva way to master writer's block, by reliving the trauma of a lost childhood, a childhood which ended long before it should have.

Matthew—he'd been Matt in those days—had just turned six very short years old when he stumbled out of his dark hiding place and fell across the body of his father, who had been bludgeoned to death.

Driven into the shadows by the threat of evil, Matthew had heard every blow, every scream for mercy, every wild expletive in return. But strangely enough, the sound of death wasn't what haunted him. Nor was it the smell of blood that still lingered in his memory when his thoughts turned unbidden to that time. To this day, it was the sticky sweet aroma of fresh pine sawdust that still made his stomach turn.

Matthew swallowed hard.

His father had been working in the workshop earlier that day, building a secret project for Christmas. A disobedient Matt sneaked in, hoping to get a purloined look at what he suspected was nothing more than some old dollhouse for his sister, Carol. Instead, he'd discovered a large toy chest, partially painted in glossy red enamel. His father had painstakingly carved M-A-T into the wooden lid. A slash of darker red marked the first stroke of the next *T*, an indicator that blood, sweat and perhaps even some tears had been shed over its construction.

But approaching voices meant that Matt was in danger of being discovered. He knew his father could capriciously decide that a disobedient child didn't deserve such a special gift. So rather than be discovered,

Matthew hid in the most convenient place at hand—the toy chest. He held his breath when he heard the harsh voices. He covered his mouth, stifling his own screams to keep them from mingling with his father's.

Matthew remained in the chest until sunset, until the fear of darkness exceeded the fear of discovery.

That's when he'd discovered his father's body.

That's when he'd discovered the red stain on his hands.

Paint or blood?

He wasn't sure.

But that was the moment when his life had changed.

And he wasn't the only person who changed. His mother changed. His sister had changed.

Matthew forced himself to push back from his desk, to tear his gaze away from the words on the monitor.

And now Danny's life would change.

They were kindred souls, he and Danny, stained by violence. Danny would have moments of near suffocation that only Matthew could understand. No matter how caring, no matter how involved, no matter how much Jill Kincaid would want to soothe away her son's irrational fears, she simply wouldn't understand. Danny needed someone who understood what the sight of extreme, personal violence could do a young boy. He needed someone who knew how to lance the wound before it festered.

Matthew glanced at the clock on his desk, appalled to see that it was almost nine o'clock in the morning. He'd expected the police to make an appearance or call before now. Danny's mom might be able to address the child's immediate needs for comfort and love, but Matthew knew what else he needed.

He picked up the phone and dialed.

"Hello, Jeff? I need your help."

"WE DON'T NEED A LAWYER, Mr. Childs. We haven't done anything wrong."

"Please, call me Matthew."

Jill wrapped the blanket around her legs, unable to ward off the chilled air that made her shake. At least it seemed more acceptable if she could blame her shivers on the temperature of the room.

For the moment, Danny seemed to have pushed back the terrors of the night. He sat on the floor, watching cartoons. She'd found him there, engrossed, when she'd woken up on the couch. For one wild moment, she'd thought she'd lost him, that her empty arms would stay empty. But the sounds of cartoon voices and Danny's hesitant giggle filled her heart with a flood of renewed faith and joy.

She looked into solemn, brown eyes, then remembered where she was and why she was there. And who this man was. Her host. Carol's brother. The man suggesting that she needed a lawyer.

"A l-lawyer…"

He continued, "I'm not saying you've done anything illegal. On the contrary, a lawyer will protect Danny's rights as a witness."

"As a witness?" She stared at her beautiful son, who, for the moment, looked as if nothing out of the ordinary had occurred in his small world. "But you told me he didn't see anything."

"They don't think he did, but how can they be sure until they question him?"

"Question him?" she repeated, feeling her skin prickle. "You mean interrogate him?"

Matthew shook his head. "No, nothing like that.

But even though Sid Morrison is a good cop, he's used to questioning adults, teenagers on occasion, but not a young, impressionable child like Danny.''

''Impressionable.'' The word snagged her attention. ''By that, you mean Danny might say something that's not true merely to impress a policeman?''

''Or you. Or maybe the opposite.'' Beneath a stray lock of dark hair, the man's brows furrowed. ''Danny might hold something back if he thought it would make someone mad at him. The trick is to get the truth out of Danny without adding to the emotional trauma he's already suffering. After all, the child just lost his father. He must be devastated.''

A giggle rose from Danny as he reacted to the television.

Jill almost smiled. ''He doesn't sound too devastated at the moment, does he?''

Matthew shrugged. ''It'll hit him at odd times. And you'll need to be prepared.'' He paused and stared at her, his piercing concern making a shiver dance across the back of her neck. ''What about you? How are you holding up?''

Jill wrapped the blanket a little tighter. ''Pretty good. After all, it's not like we were married, or anything.''

''You were, at one time.''

She busied herself with the loose threads from a frayed corner of the blanket. ''For about a minute and a half. Long enough for me to realize what sort of scum he was.'' She paused and added in a darker voice, ''And long enough for me to get pregnant.'' She wrapped the thread around her forefinger. ''That man was never meant to father children. He's not...wasn't more than an overgrown child himself.

But you must know all about that. He married your sister, right?'' Jill straightened quickly, realizing that she and Danny weren't the only ones who were suffering because of the situation. "How is your sister, anyway?"

The light of concern in Matthew's eyes was virtually extinguished. "I don't know. I haven't called the hospital, yet."

Jill felt herself flush. Here she'd been so wrapped up in her own misery that she'd monopolized his time and prevented him from paying attention to his own problems—mainly his sister, who, according to the police, had been seriously injured. "I'm so sorry. You've been concentrating on Danny and me when you probably want to go to the hospital to be with your sister. Danny and I will—"

"No." He spoke with quiet force. "We don't have that kind of relationship."

For a man who had spoken with such eloquent emotion about the health and welfare of her son, a total stranger, Matthew grew as passionless as granite.

"But she's your sister," Jill offered weakly, not knowing what else to say.

He remained unnaturally stiff. "We haven't seen or spoken with each other in years."

Jill glanced down and spotted his hand drawn up in a tight fist. It was his only real manifestation of emotion, belying the cold words and empty stare.

"Sorry. I didn't mean to pry." Silence hung about them like a wet blanket, pierced only by the muted sounds of Danny's cartoon.

Matthew drew in a sharp breath, then glanced at his fist as if noticing for the first time how it betrayed the inner man. He deliberately unclenched it.

"That's okay." He managed a halfhearted smile and scanned the room as if realizing where they were. "Jeez, I'm not much of a host, am I? You hungry?" He didn't wait for an answer and turned to Danny, who was squatting on the floor in front of the television, hugging his knees. "Hey sport, you hungry? I make some mighty fine pancakes."

Danny didn't answer. He remained motionless in front of the television.

"Danny, Mr. Childs is talking to you." It only took a moment for Jill to realize that something other than the television had usurped her son's attention. She squatted on his other side and shook his shoulder lightly. "Earth to Danny…"

He seemed to have a hard time tearing his gaze away from whatever he clutched in his fist. A small shudder coursed through his body, then he looked up. "Yeah, Mom?"

"Whatcha got, sweetie?"

He uncurled his hand and held out his treasure for her inspection. "My army man."

"Oh." The next logical question would be to ask Danny where he got the toy, especially since she knew he didn't have any plastic soldiers at home. But when Jill glanced up, she locked solemn gazes with Matthew, who silently mouthed the most likely answer: the toy came from Danny's father. And the last thing Jill wanted to do at this moment was deliberately remind Danny of his father.

She attempted a hearty smile, knowing she was failing, miserably. "Danny, Mr. Childs asked you a question. Are you hungry?"

"For what?" Danny's dark eyebrows narrowed. "For Aunt Didi's grits?" He made a face, revealing what he thought of his Aunt Didi's grits. Living a single-parent, suburban car-pool life, their breakfast had never been raised above the ranks of cold cereal and toast except for those days when he stayed with with his Great-aunt Didi who still believed breakfast was a four-course meal which started with a heaping bowl of lumpy, tasteless grits.

Matthew read Danny's expression correctly. "Grits? Not in my house." The man rubbed his hands together briskly. "How do pancakes sound? Hot steamy pancakes drenched in syrup."

Danny's gritty expression faded away. "Pakes?" A new gleam replaced his previous faraway look. "I love pakes."

Matthew turned to Jill. "Pakes..." he said, as if testing the word. "I like that. Short but sweet." He grinned at Danny. "Just like you."

Jill ruffled her son's hair. "Danny talks shorthand, sometimes."

Matthew held out his hand. "Then c'mon, buddy. Let's you and me make some pakes."

To Jill's surprise, Danny slipped his hand in Matthew's, rose, and both of them headed off into the kitchen, her son never once turning back to see if his mother was following.

This, from a child who screamed for the first three weeks of prekindergarten. A child whose weekly reports charted his struggle with overwhelming separation anxiety. A child who clung to her hand as if he were glued to it when they shopped. A child who begged and pleaded to forgo the court-ordered visitation periods with a father he feared with the same intensity that he feared Darth Vader.

How wonderfully odd to see her precious, precocious Danny, blithely slipping his hand into a strange man's and skipping happily away.

A breakthrough?

Or a breakdown?

How would she be able to tell the difference?

LOOP DE LOOP.

Going around in circles.

You would have thought grown men might have found a better way of making a living. But that was the sort of lifestyle that always appealed to wild young men with no sense of their own mortality.

Life in the fast lane.

High speeds.

Fancy cars.

Not to mention the constant need for competition between two brothers.

I stared at the page dedicated to the memories of these deaths. The laminated card fixed there read McCreedy Pit Crew Pass. Pits of hell of was more like it.

A nice smudge of brown-gold filled the bottom left corner of the page and a darker splotch filled the right corner. And in the center, I pasted a picture of the two men I'd found in the newspaper. Their smirking faces were frozen in broad grins as if competing for the camera's attention.

Well, they wouldn't be competing anymore. Not on the track. Not in bed. There would be no more tiny female silhouettes painted across the hood of their cars, each symbolizing an anonymous conquest in bed.

The score—137 women versus 129. Poor Billy, trailing his brother Vernon by eight unlawfully bedded women....

But there would be no more nameless, faceless couplings that didn't even last long enough to be called one-night stands. There would be no more track chicks and no more track brats, fathered by two poor excuses for men who shared none of the blame and none of the responsibility.

I closed the scrapbook and allowed myself to savor the memories. The thunder would roll no more and the lightning would never streak the sky again.

No thanks was necessary.

Chapter Five

Jill wished she couldn't see herself in the mirror that dominated the wall behind Lieutenant Morrison. Until that moment, she thought she'd been able to control her expressions, hide her fear and concern, all for Danny's sake. But one casual glance at her own reflection shattered her illusions of composure.

She looked frightened.

And perhaps even a little guilty.

But that was understandable, wasn't it? After all, the biggest complication in her life, her ex-husband, was now gone. No more arguments. No more word games, mind games. She drew in a sharp breath of air that tasted like stale cigarettes.

No more tug-of-war.

Luckily, Morrison wasn't paying much attention to her, but instead, directed his questions to her son. However, Jill was bright enough to know even if the lieutenant wasn't watching her, others were. That was no ordinary mirror. There were people sitting behind it, observing her with care, judging her by the expressions on her face, by her body language, by whatever method the police used to gauge truth and honesty by sight.

Perhaps that was the most frightening thing of all.

"So tell me about your dad, Danny." Morrison stuffed his hand in his jacket pocket and pulled out a couple of small wooden blocks which he lined up on the scarred table. Up to now, they'd chitchatted about school, friends, bringing up all sorts of innocuous topics obviously chosen to make Danny more comfortable and establish a rapport between cop and witness. To his credit, Morrison seemed to know how to relate to a child; he'd even played with Danny's toy soldier, making the appropriate percussive noises that seemed endemic to war games.

His smile even seemed genuine. "What did you and your Dad do yesterday?"

Danny stared at the blocks. "Nuffin'."

"Nothing?" Morrison produced another block and stacked it on top of the other blocks. "On a Saturday? You didn't even watch cartoons in the morning?"

Danny shrugged. "Aunt Carol was going to let me watch 'Omega Rangers,' but Daddy said we didn't have time. We had to run errands."

"Run errands," Morrison repeated, pulling out another block. This time he flipped it across the table toward Danny, but her son didn't automatically reach out and catch it. The block landed close to the others without hitting them. After a brief hesitation, Danny reached out and wrapped his small hand around the wooden cube.

"Where you going to put it?" Morrison prompted, nodding at the boy's hand. "Myself, I like building walls."

Danny scrutinized the fledgling foundation. "I like building—" he pursed his lips "—towers." He created a third level by balancing his block on the top of the other two.

"That's my second favorite thing to build." Morrison produced another block. "What kind of errands did you and your Dad run?"

Danny waited until Morrison dropped the block on the table and shifted back in his chair before reaching for it. "We had to go to his office and talk to some lady there." Danny contemplated his architecture and placed the block at the bottom of the tower to bolster the foundation.

Jill smiled in spite of herself. Her son, the engineer.

The lieutenant nodded his approval at the block's placement. "His office? The one at the radio station?"

Danny reached out in time to accept the block directly from the lieutenant. Another block—another level of the tower. "Uh-huh. I like going to the station. The engineer let me run the board while Daddy and the lady talked."

"Run the board? I thought engineers ran trains." Morrison flipped Danny another block and turned to Jill for explanation. "What does he mean?"

Jill swallowed hard, then instantly regretted the action as if it betrayed some sort of secret guilt. *I've done nothing wrong...other than be naive enough—stupid enough—to marry Bummpt.* "Uh...each broadcasting studio has a control site where they monitor the sound levels, patch in telephone calls, play carts...er...cartridges with sound effects, music, commercials...stuff like that."

Danny looked up from his intense study of the tower's structure. "I played the 'burp' cart over and over and over and the engineer laughed."

Morrison raised an eyebrow. "They let a kid control what was being broadcast on the radio?"

Jill shook her head. "If it was the Bummpt studio, they weren't on the air. My ex-husband's show runs…ran weeknights from eight to midnight."

Morrison nodded and turned back to Danny again. "Tell me about the lady your dad was talking to."

Danny faced Jill, his face screwed up in perplexed thought. "Don't 'member her name, but I 'member she doesn't like kids."

Jill thought for a moment. "Was it a lady with short black hair or long curly red hair?"

Danny nodded. "The red hair lady. The one with the click-click shoes."

Jill glanced up at the lieutenant. "Lisa Crenshaw," she explained, "the producer of the show. She's been with Bummpt for several years." She paused for a moment. "She wears heels. Stilettos."

Morrison gave Danny another block. "So your dad and this Crenshaw lady were just talking while you were playing with the controls?"

Danny gave his tower a long, appraising glance, then placed the block at its base rather than on the teetering top. "Nope."

Another block.

Morrison pushed back in his chair and stifled a yawn. "What do you mean, 'Nope'?"

Danny made a face as if to say, *You idiot, don't you understand?* "I could see them through the glass."

"The glass?" Another block.

Danny swiveled in his seat and gave Jill an imploring look as if to say, *You explain it. I can't.*

She nodded. "The control booth has a large observation window so the engineer can see what's happening in the broadcasting studio.'' It took all her control not to look up at the mirror and acknowledge its similar role.

''Daddy and the lady were fighting,'' Danny offered.

Morrison turned his attention back to another block. ''Fighting? As in hitting and punching each other?''

Danny continued to study his handiwork. ''Nope, adult fighting. At first I couldn't hear them—''

Jill interrupted quickly. ''The studios are soundproof.''

Danny nodded. ''But I hit a button on the board and then I could hear them yelling, screaming and using bad words.'' His little face darkened for a moment. ''Just like Momma and Daddy used to do.'' He straightened suddenly, concern flooding his face as he realized the implications he was making. ''But Momma never used the bad words. Ever!''

Morrison gave her a quick glance. ''I'm sure she never did.''

Jill almost believed him.

The lieutenant turned around and rewarded Danny with two blocks which her son used to form a wider base for his tower. ''So,'' the lieutenant continued, ''your dad and Lisa Crenshaw argued about something—we don't know what. What happened next?''

Danny pursed his lips in the effort to remember. ''The engineer hit another button and we couldn't hear them anymore. Then he put in another cart which sounded like...'' His voice faded away and he reddened visibly. ''Momma doesn't like me to say the word.''

Morrison leaned forward in obvious conspiracy. ''What word?''

Danny shot Jill a sidelong glance, then leaned forward as well, cupping his hands to his mouth, as if to direct the sound to the policeman's ears only, but Danny hadn't quite mastered the art of whispering. "Like someone farted."

Morrison managed to hide his grin. "I won't tell her you said that, okay, sport?" He sat back in his chair. "And then what happened?"

Danny mimicked his movements, sliding back in his chair until his legs stretched out straight in front of him. "We went to McDonald's and had ice cream for lunch."

Jill closed her eyes. *Ice cream? For lunch?* Her ex-husband had always bounced between catering to his son's every unspoken whim and ignoring the child for months on end. When it came to visitation time, neither she nor Danny knew which Daniel would meet them at the door: Disneyland Dan or Deadbeat Dad. What he never understood was that a trip to McDonald's was probably on the same level as a trip to the Magic Kingdom from Danny's perspective.

Her son's solemn voice cut through her thoughts. "But I made Daddy buy me a Happy Meal first." There was an uncomfortable pause and then he spoke again. "Daddy called me a party pooper."

Jill opened her eyes in time to see her son's crestfallen pout. Anger began to flow through her veins. How dare Daniel McFadden chastise her son for being more mature than his own father? At only four years old, Danny showed more judgment and sense of compassion than his father as an adult could ever wring from his perforated personality and warped identity. If she had her way, Bummpt would never again be allowed to—

A shiver coursed through her body. That would no longer be a problem, now. Bummpt was dead. No more visitations, no more snide remarks, no more arguments about the right way to raise a McFadden male.

The King of Radio Sleaze is dead.

Long live the King.

Jill slipped her hand into her son's and gave it a squeeze. Now it was just the two of them. And she couldn't be more relieved.

Morrison handed Danny another block. "So, what did you do after lunch?"

Jill swallowed back the worst of her emotion. The adage "And life goes on" danced through her head.

Danny squinted at his tower and then placed the block gently on top. "We drove around in Daddy's new car."

Another new car. Jill tried not to wince. When he presented her the monthly check, Bummpt always acted as if every dollar he paid in child support deprived him of some necessity of life…like leather interior. He had a new car and she was driving a used station wagon on its last legs.

"You drove around." Morrison handed Danny another piece of wood. "Where?"

Danny waited until he positioned the block before shrugging. "I don't 'member. Just places. I stayed in the car, mostly."

Morrison glanced at Jill and raised one eyebrow. For once, she felt as if the censuring expression the man wore was directed at Bummpt, not at her.

Morrison turned back to Danny. "What about that night? At dinnertime?"

Danny studied his masterpiece. "We had pizza." He started making minor adjustments to his design.

"Pepperoni?"

"Nope." Danny didn't even look up from his reconstruction project. "Black olive." The green plastic soldier made a reappearance and Danny found a hiding place for him within the structure.

The lieutenant made a face. "Black olives? Yuck. Your Dad must have ordered it."

Danny shook his head. "Nope, Aunt Carol did. She 'membered black olive's my favorite. Then after I finished, she made me take a bath—" he made a face which faded quickly into an embarrassed grin "—then she read me a bedtime story. She'd bought me a new book while I was with Daddy."

Jill closed her eyes again. Up to now, she'd dismissed Carol Childs McFadden as the last in a line of flashy, empty-headed girlfriends, the big winner who coerced Bummpt into turning her into his newest trophy wife. But now after meeting Matthew and learning this little choice bit of information from Danny, maybe there was more to the woman than rushed to meet the eye at their first rather awkward meeting.

Jill hadn't been impressed with the peroxided hair, the artificially enhanced body or the way Carol wrapped herself possessively around Bummpt's thigh. The first time they met, the woman had damned near growled at Jill as if she'd been a threat to the blissful newlyweds.

But evidently, Carol had occasionally filled the void left behind by Bummpt, who couldn't be trusted to feed his son, bathe him or put him to bed.

Danny's small voice pricked her attention. "I like Aunt Carol." There was a long pause before he spoke again, his voice small and full of concern. "Is she going to die, too?"

Jill pulled her son into her lap. "I don't think so, honey. Aunt Carol is at the hospital where the doctors are going to do their best to make her well again."

He nodded as if her reassurance was enough to banish his fears.

Morrison held out a block. "Do you remember what happened after your Aunt Carol put you to bed?"

Danny contemplated the block for a long moment before making the decision to reach out and take it. "Mr. Popster and I told each other stories and then I fell asleep."

The lieutenant looked up at Jill. "Mr. Popster?"

"A stuffed..." She bit her lip. What did you call it? It wasn't a stuffed animal in the traditional sense, at least not a recognizable animal. Time and the washing machine had long ago robbed the toy of its identifying animal characteristics. And if she referred to it as a doll in front of Danny, who knows what his reaction would be? Thanks to his father, who thought it had been cute to teach their son some key chauvinistic phrases, calling Mr. Popster a doll became a federal offense since "boys don't play with dolls." Luckily, Danny had picked up only the rhetoric, not the philosophy, and Mr. Popster, be he a doll or a stuffed whatever, was a valued member of the family and Danny's constant companion, especially at bedtime.

Before Jill could formulate an answer, Danny provided the perfect solution. He held up his worn toy by one bedraggled arm. "This is Mr. Popster."

Morrison nodded. "Please to meetcha, Pops." He held out his palm, complete with wooden block.

Danny snatched it with glee. "He can't stack stuff."

He waved Mr. Popster's truncated hand at the policeman. "No fingers."

Morrison broke out in a brief smile. "Oh." The expression faded. "So you and The Popster slept all night?" Another block.

"*Mister* Popster," Danny corrected. "And we woke up when we heard the noise."

"Noise?" Another block.

Danny squirmed in Jill's lap. "A loud noise. A really loud noise. The loudest noise you ever heard in your entire life." After a moment, he leaned forward and placed one of the blocks gingerly on the top level. The tower teetered for a moment, but maintained its shape. He clutched the other block in his small hand.

"Loud?" Morrison leaned forward. "Like thunder?"

Danny turned toward Jill, his eyes wide. "Th-thunder?" A sudden tear trickled down his cheek. "Is that what killed Daddy? Thunder? I'm scared of thunder...."

Jill's heart stopped in midbeat, making her draw in a sharp stinging breath. Her baby. Her sweet, sweet baby...

But his father's son, too.

Only a scant moment later, Danny stiffened, wiping his tears on the back of his fist. He stared at his damp hand, then uncurled it to reveal his last block. With an expression which was eerily reminiscent of his late father's, he hurled the block at the tower he had so carefully constructed around his toy soldier and in a voice which was merely a younger, higher pitched version of Bumppt's, he yelled, "Party pooper!"

The tower collapsed.

And with it, went Jill's self-control.

MATTHEW WATCHED the blocks of wood scattered across the table. *Strategic error, Sid.* Judging by the look on the lieutenant's face, it took only a moment for Sid to realize it, too.

All that work—all the trust he'd built, block by block with Danny. All of it destroyed because of an unfortunate word selection.

Thunder.

Matthew shook his head. If Danny wasn't afraid of thunder and lightning before, he certainly would be now.

The man sitting next to Matthew, Barnaby "Cotton" McNeil reached up and switched off the speaker which had allowed them to hear the conversation in the next room. The sounds of a child's sorrow were magically silenced.

If only sorrow could be as easily ended with the flip of a switch.

Even though Matthew could no longer hear Jill, her sadness radiated through the two-way mirror as plainly as her anger shone in her face. He knew exactly what she was feeling and saying to herself; how dare they force her only child to go through all this again, to face the memories of last night's fear? If she only knew how much more healthy it was to let the child purge some of the sorrow from his system through a cathartic session like this.

Cotton lit a cigar and exhaled slowly. "Boy's not going to tell us anything else, now."

Matthew found his voice after a moment. "I still think she should have had a lawyer present at the questioning."

"Jeez, it's not like we thought the kid did it or sumpin' like that," he drawled. "And Mom's alibi seems relatively solid, too. She'd been having some single parents meeting at her house. She has a group of twenty-odd women and all of 'em are ready to swear she was there with them until eleven. We figure there's no way she could have driven here in two hours, offed ol' Bummpt in the Night and driven back in time to be there when the locals came to break the bad news. Just ain't possible.'' Cotton took another long draw on his cigar. "That is…if the ladies are telling the truth. A bunch of dee-vorced women…they tend to close ranks, you know, protect their own.…''

"You actually think they'd lie to help her cover up a murder?'' Matthew couldn't keep the incredulity out of his voice.

Cotton shrugged. "Probably not.'' He brightened briefly. "Oh course, that doesn't mean she didn't hire someone to whack the guy.'' Cotton studied her through the glass. "You ever listen to her husband on the radio?''

"Ex-husband,'' Matthew corrected. "And no, I'm not into shock radio.''

Cotton flicked a small amount of ash onto the floor. "I gotta admit ol' 'Bummpt in the Night' was a funny sum-bitch, in a sorta raw way. Lord, that man would say anything to rile people and get them to call in, cussing and a-fussing. I heard someone say that not only was Bummpt willing to turn a sacred cow into a sacred burger, but he'd even find some vegetarians to eat it in front of.''

Matthew stared at Danny. "Sounds like perfect father material.''

Cotton's cigar bobbed as he spoke. "You know Bummpt used to talk all the time on the radio about his ex-wife and their divorce. He made her sound like a cross between a female gorilla and...that whatcha-macallit mythological creature with the snakes in her hair.''

''A Medusa,'' Matthew supplied, unable to tear his gaze away from mother and son.

''Yeah, a Medusa.'' Cotton crossed his arms as smoke rose to ring his head with a gray halo. ''Funny, but she—'' he nodded toward the window ''—wasn't what I expected at all. I sorta expected ol' Bummpt to have him a real looker, someone younger, sexier, racier....'' He offered Matthew a red-faced grin. ''Someone sluttier...''

Matthew stood, his self-control hanging on for dear life as a red-hot flood of emotion made his fists tighten and his ears buzz. For a moment, he wasn't sure who he was mad at—Cotton or Bummpt.

Cotton turned a dusky red. ''Oh, jeez, man...your sister. I...I wasn't thinking. I didn't mean it like that. I swear.''

Matthew turned away from the man, unwilling to acknowledge the stuttered apology, mainly because it brought up a good point: what sort of woman married a man like Daniel ''Bummpt'' McFadden?

Matthew knew enough about the business to realize that a man's radio persona didn't necessarily reflect his real personality, in most cases.

But this wasn't just any case. This was ''Bummpt in the Night,'' a man who had created a legend filled with unbelievable sexual exploits, a notorious man who created an impossible reputation then strived to fulfill it.

His fist tightened. *Carol, if I'd known you were going to marry the man, I might have killed the bastard myself.*

Chapter Six

They drove back in silence punctuated only by an occasional sniffing noise. Since Matthew was driving and his passengers had opted to sit—that is, huddle—together in the back seat, he didn't know which one was crying—Jill or her son. When he turned around in his seat to announce their arrival, he learned that Danny was asleep and Jill had been the one crying.

She hastily wiped her eyes as she looked around. "I thought you were going to take us to a hotel."

He nodded toward his house. "Wouldn't you be more comfortable here?"

She stared at his front door for a long moment before answering. "Yes," she whispered. "We probably would."

He knew he had to lighten her damp mood a little. "Of course, the room service isn't as good." He got out of the car and opened her door. "But I'm a whiz at handling baggage." He leaned down. "And speaking of baggage...let me take Danny. I already know that he weighs a ton when he's asleep."

For a moment, he was afraid she wasn't going to let go of her child. But with a small sigh, she unbuckled Danny's seat belt, then grunted as she hoisted him across her lap and passed him through the open door to Matthew. Danny roused for a moment, realized who had him, then nuzzled closer.

Jill looked surprised. "He really likes you."

Matthew smiled, shifting the child's dead weight in his arms. "It's mutual. Danny's a great kid."

Jill closed the door softly. "Isn't this a little fast? After all, you barely know him."

The look she gave him was almost accusatory, as if he were motivated by something other than altruism. He could understand that; tragedy had its own set of rules and until you'd lived through a similar situation, you weren't quite sure what those rules were. He tried to smile. "You know the old saying—'There are no atheists in foxholes.'"

Jill remained silent until they got into the house. She stopped at the couch, but dutifully followed Matthew as he passed through the living room and down the hallway to the guest room. He paused, allowing Jill to reach the bed before him.

"I don't know if he'll like this when he wakes up," she whispered as she pulled back the bedspread.

"Maybe this'll help." He tucked Mr. Popster into Danny's arms. The child pulled the stuffed toy closer to his chest and hugged it with a reaction born out of instinct.

Jill leaned down to kiss her sleeping son. When she straightened, Matthew could see exhaustion blanketing her features. Exhaustion, worry and sadness. He'd seen a similar look on his mother's face but there was a difference. For all her troubles, Jill didn't look helpless. Matthew's mother surrendered early on to the emotions that eroded her soul and turned her into a zombie. Somehow, Jill looked as if she wouldn't go down without a fight.

She hesitated at the door, giving her son one more lingering glance. "I'm going to leave the door open— so I can hear him if he wakes up."

Matthew nodded. "He'll sleep for a while." He paused and took inventory of her pinched features, her pale skin and her uneasy stance. "You know he's not the only one who looks tired."

She sighed. "I feel like I'll never sleep again."

Matthew recognized all too well that feeling of exhaustion—the type that weighed too heavily on the mind to allow it to shut down. The gears would keep turning, grinding until the brain burned out and the body collapsed. He thought of his own mother. And some people never made it back to their feet after they fell.

He glanced at Jill, seeing the lines that tension and fear had etched near her eyes. Then he remembered Danny's face, the terror as he destroyed his tower and threw himself at his mother. Up to that point, Matthew could only sporadically see the child due to the angle of his chair. But when Danny turned his face to the mirror, Matthew didn't see fear and confusion. He saw anger. Pure, red-hot anger.

A familiar anger.

That was why fate had dumped all this in his lap— part of being a survivor was helping others to learn to survive and cope with the fear, the confusion and especially the anger. And if he was going to try to help Danny, the first person he had to help was his mother.

"You need something to eat. That's the standard procedure after the police grill you—you grill something in return.'' He offered her his most endearing smile. "Like grilled cheese sandwiches?"

Wait.

This didn't sound like the type of altruistic help he'd espoused just a moment ago. It sounded more like...flirting. Matthew performed a quick analysis of his motives.

Was he flirting?

Was he seriously trying to make time with the Widow McFadden?

An ugly shiver crawled up his back. What sort of scum was he? He should be at the hospital, checking on Carol in person, rather than making impersonal calls to the nursing station where they kept repeating, "Serious condition but improving.'' He should be keeping some sort of vigil. He should be—

"Normally, I'd say yes," Jill continued, unaware of the thoughts trampling through his head. She even managed a pasty grin of her own which faded quickly. "But I think the definition of the word *normal* has changed radically for me in the past twenty-four hours."

He nodded, pushing back the worst of the accusations that swam through his thoughts. An unending series of questions with no answers was a sure indicator of his own level of stress. How many times after the murder had endless series of irrational "what ifs" led him straight into a full-blown panic?

He distracted himself by gesturing for her to follow him. But he couldn't help but philosophize a bit along the way. "When something like this happens to you, you look at the whole world in a completely different light."

She gave him a quizzical look as they entered the

kitchen. "You sound as if you've gone through this before."

What did he tell her? His own sob story? Would it make her feel better? Probably not. Somehow he didn't think she needed to hear that it took almost six years to identify his father's killer, another fourteen to catch the man. And another six for him to come to grips with the role he'd played in identifying the murderer. But that was the purpose of Matthew's book— to exorcise the last of the demons that had filled the space where happy childhood memories should have been.

Suddenly, he had an urge to forget food and return to his computer. To write. To purge his soul…

He glanced at Jill and checked the urge.

Lucky for her, there were only two souls involved this tragic time. Hers and Danny's. Selfishly, Matthew was glad he didn't need to mourn. All he had to do was purge his guilt over the gulf that time and circumstance had placed between him and his sister.

Then he remembered. Carol had a stake in this tragedy, too. That made three souls touched by Bummpt's violent death. Seeing how Carol had never quite recovered from their father's death, how would she cope with the death of her husband? Had she changed enough in six years to handle this situation without falling apart? And if she needed help, would she turn to him?

He answered his own question: *Probably not.*

They'd gotten used to holding each other at arm's length. Somewhere down the line, they began measuring their distance by feet, then by yards and eventually by miles. Now, they were indeed miles apart.

And those miles had made him a lousy brother and her a lousy sister.

They deserved each other, he guessed.

He swallowed hard and redirected his wandering mind, forcing himself to concentrate on a less mundane concern: food. He hauled bread, butter and cheese from his refrigerator, grateful to see that Mrs. Flynn had replenished all of them. He looked around. Where was Mrs. F., anyway? He glanced back at the refrigerator and spotted a yellow sticky note on the freezer door.

"Gone to hospital. Be back at 2."

The hospital.

Good ol' Mrs. Flynn. She cooked for him, cleaned for him, kept the sock drawer organized, stayed out of his office except to retrieve a daily armload of dirty dishes. She took care of everything, all his responsibilities. Evidently, even his familial ones.

"...you okay?"

Matthew felt a light touch on his arm and looked up, startled to see Jill standing next to him, concern crowding the fatigue in her face. How could he have forgotten she was there? He started to speak, then stopped, as he found himself entranced by the look of tired strength in her eyes.

For a moment, they connected as two people sharing one tragedy. Suddenly he saw things from her perspective, feeling her sense of helplessness and fear and her love for her son. And he sensed the strong core at the center of her being, the tenacious part of her soul that would keep her from snapping under the weight of the calamity that had struck her life.

And for the briefest flash, jealousy surged through him.

Why couldn't his own mother have dealt with the tragedy like that? When his father died, Matthew ended up losing two parents, one to a switchblade, the other to grief. Only his mother didn't immediately depart this world and instead walked around as an empty shell, so self-absorbed by her loss that she forgot the others who remained behind—Matthew and Carol.

Guilt stabbed at him, again. *Carol.*

"I feel terrible." Jill glanced down at the note he cradled in his palm. "You haven't seen your sister yet because Danny and I have been monopolizing your time. Why don't you go now? We'll be okay by ourselves."

Matthew wadded up the note into a small yellow ball. Funny, but his stomach felt as if it had been wadded up in the same way. "Carol's got company. Mrs. Flynn, my housekeeper, is visiting her."

"Don't you think she…er…Carol would rather see her brother?"

Matthew ripped open the middle of the bread bag and pulled out four slices of bread. "Don't bet on it. Carol doesn't want much to do with me."

Jill studied the torn bread bag longer than he liked. Then she lifted her eyes and caught him in a solemn gaze. "But she called you. Right after the…attack, she called you. If she didn't want to see you, why would she have called?"

Matthew fished around for the skillet that sat inconveniently in the middle of the pile of pots and pans. Somehow the rattling noise seemed to help express in action what he couldn't in words. Finally, he freed the pan and placed it on the stove eye with more of a bang than he'd really intended.

"Carol wasn't calling me. She was calling the

house.'' He glanced ruefully around the kitchen. ''We moved here shortly after my father died and this is where I grew up. She was hurt and confused and she did what seemed natural at the moment—she called home.'' He shrugged. ''I just happen to still live here. Anyway—'' he nodded toward the refrigerator ''—my housekeeper is the best person to be with Carol right now. She was the closest thing we had to a mother when we were growing up.'' Even when Carol changed so radically, she never severed the ties with Mrs. F.

''I bet she'd still like you to visit.''

He shook his head. ''If I went, we'd end up arguing and that can't be good for her, in the condition she's in.''

Jill's face darkened perceptibly. ''Do you hate her that much for marrying Bummpt?''

A surge of remorse cut through Matthew as easily as the knife bit into his finger. ''That's not it.'' He glanced down at the drop of blood filling the thin slit in his index fingertip. ''I didn't even know she'd gotten married, much less to…'' He paused, his reporter's instincts on alert. ''You call him 'Bummpt.' Isn't that a little odd?''

She drew a deep breath. ''I married Daniel McFadden, but I divorced 'Bummpt in the Night.' Somewhere along the line, his personality changed and his radio persona took over.'' She leaned against the counter. ''I could put up with a lot, but I couldn't put up with Bummpt.'' Her face darkened. ''And I couldn't have someone like Bummpt raising my child.''

''You make it sound as if he were two different people.''

"He was." She reached over and began to position the slices of cheese on the bread. "The man I met always had a wild streak—he was sometimes unpredictable but he was also whimsical, fun. That's what I thought I needed in my life. Fun. But when he got the night gig, it triggered something in him and his wild streak changed. He got louder, meaner, more controlling of those around him, but at the same time, he himself became very erratic. It became dangerous to stick around so I split."

"But you let Danny visit his father."

She shook her head. "No, the court let Danny visit his father. If it had been up to me, Bummpt would have remained a faceless voice on the radio." She swallowed hard. "It scares me to death every time I send Danny up here to visit for a weekend. Bummpt likes…liked to teach him phrases that no four-year old should know or even hear. It takes nearly two weeks to…to deprogram Danny and erase or, at least, counteract all the 'lessons' his father has taught him.

"Lessons? Like what?"

"You know—the usual. The subservient role of women to men. The supremacy of one race over another. Every chauvinistic or bigoted concept you can imagine." She stared off into space, her eyes vacant, but one hand tightened into a fist. "That's what Bummpt thought was fun to teach his son." She paused, then corrected herself. "My son."

Matthew's stomach turned. And this was the type of man his sister had chosen to marry? Had she been that desperate for an authoritative male figure in her life? How could she listen to someone like that? Or live with him?

How could she love him?

A thought floated in the back of his mind. Maybe she didn't love him. Maybe the police had to look no further for Bummpt's murderer than his wife.

He glanced up at Jill, then down to her clenched fist.

Or his ex-wife?

Jill locked gazes with him, reading the doubt in his face. She reached over and turned off the stove burner. "I don't think either of us want to eat right now." She was no fool. She realized what he was thinking. Either his sister or his houseguest was a murderer.

Jill watched as he pivoted then walked blindly out of the kitchen, past the living room and down the hallway. She trailed behind him, not quite sure he was even aware of her. Then again, if he honestly thought she was a murderer, how could he not be painfully aware of her presence?

He went past the room where Danny was sleeping, then paused at a darkened doorway.

Jill reached out and touched him.

He jumped.

"I didn't kill Bummpt," she offered in a soft voice.

"I know." He stepped into the room and reached for the wall switch. "Believe me, I know a murderer when I see one."

Harsh light filled the room.

She took an involuntary gasp of air.

Pictures and newspaper clippings covered every wall of the room except one. The remaining wall was strangely bare except for a random pattern of white splotches, as if it had once held the same sort of memorabilia as the others but had been stripped of its decorations. She held her breath as she looked at the closest picture, that of a chalk outline on a wooden floor and a dark stain at the figure's head. It took a moment for her to realize that black-and-white film had made the blood look more like...

"Ink." Matthew unpinned a photograph from the wall. "It's a lot easier to think about, if you think the blood is actually ink. Which—" he emitted a rough bark of laughter "—is awfully appropriate, since my father was a printer. People always said he had ink for blood." He glanced ruefully at the picture. "They don't know how right they were."

"Your father..."

Matthew nodded. "I was a little older than Danny when my father was murdered. I've been through all of this before— the investigations, the accusations, the unending questions. I know what sort of things Danny's feeling and what he's going to go through."

"I'm...I'm sorry," Jill stuttered, not knowing what else to say.

"Don't be." He pointed to the walls and the computer setup that sat in the middle of the room "All of this is my way of coping with his death. You see...I found his murderer." A smile of fleeting satisfaction flitted across his face. "It took twenty-six years, but I found the man who killed my father and I got enough evidence to put him away for life."

Jill scanned the room. This didn't look like the office of someone who had put his troubles behind him. If the murder had been solved and the guilty party caught, then why was there such a grim legacy left behind? What sort of man wallowed in pictures of crime scenes? Of his own father, no less?

"It's not what you think." He indicated the walls with an open palm. "I'm a newspaper reporter and I'm writing about this—my father's murder and the capture of his killer, purging all this from my soul by writing a book. Now, Carol…" He pointed to a school picture of a towheaded child of ten or eleven with a strained smile and dark circles under her eyes. "Carol's the one who never got over his death. She never found an outlet for the anger and frustration so it built up inside her."

Jill tried not to look at the gruesome pictures that ringed the photo of Carol. "You think she killed Bummpt?"

Matthew shrugged. "It's possible. She was always drawn to powerful men, valuing fame and fortune over integrity and intellect. It took a lot of money to help her buy the things she needed to temporarily vent her frustrations—booze, drugs. I didn't know she'd married Bummpt but now that I've had a chance to think about it, it shouldn't surprise me. She's always been a moth looking for a flame. And I think you'd admit that Bummpt is…was a pretty fiery type of guy. I'm sure his fame was part of the attraction."

Jill couldn't help but make a face. "Fame isn't all what it's cracked up to be. Neither was Bummpt. He was more like a volcano than a torch."

"My sister always liked to play at the edge, to dance along the rim of disaster." He sighed. "She was out of control by time she was a teenager. When she got older, she started getting in trouble with the law—small crimes growing into bigger ones. She'd hang around the wrong sort and get caught up in their activities. But her relationships never lasted. At least they haven't up to now. She always found a reason to have some big, wild emotional explosion and then she'd run away. Only this time, maybe the explosion wasn't so wild. Maybe it was controlled, aimed.

Maybe she took her rage out on someone, on Bummpt in a specified way…with a knife in his—''

Jill's stomach lurched and she held up her hand. ''Please…I can't handle this right now. Not in here.'' As she turned her back on his gallery of horrors and stepped into the hallway, she was aghast to learn that the mental image he'd drawn in her head refused to fade.

''I'm…sorry.'' Matthew followed her, switching off the light as he exited the room.

She swallowed back the worst of her revulsion. ''For a man who says he's gotten over a tragedy in his life, you're still strongly connected to all the details, aren't you?''

He stared at her for a moment as if no one had dared make him take such an analysis of himself. Then he slowly nodded. ''That's why I'm writing a book. It's a way of purging my soul. When I get through with each chapter, I pull down those pictures and put them away. You saw the one wall. Bare. I bared my soul, then patched the holes that had been left behind. It's quite freeing to get the story down on paper and then simply pack up your memories.''

She crossed her arms; he made it all sound too easy, too convenient. ''Can you? Can you truly pack up the memories and banish mental images like that?''

''With help, you can.'' He stepped closer to her. ''That's why I want to recommend that you get Danny some help.''

''Help?'' She felt the muscles in her arms tighten. ''What sort of help?''

Matthew glanced down the hallway toward the room where Danny slept. ''I think he saw more than we might know, but the trauma of what he saw is keeping him from telling us.''

She followed his gaze, then felt a cold chill run down her neck. ''Us?''

''You, me, the police. There are two very good reasons for getting someone to help Danny remember what he saw.'' He held up his hand and ticked off the points. ''One—if he saw his father's body, that's a big burden for a child to carry without having someone help him sort through his feelings.'' He stared at his hand, held out the second finger then hesitated.

''And?'' she prompted.

''Two—if Danny did see who killed his father, his life may be in dan—''

A shrill cry filled the air. At first, Matthew thought it was Jill, but realized a split second later, it came from the bedroom.

Matthew always thought he had quick reactions, but a mother's instincts proved to be infinitely faster. Before he could move, Jill had bolted down the hall, headed to her son. Matthew struggled to stay one step behind her and by the time he'd skidded into the guest room, he found Jill and Danny huddling in a shadowy corner.

''It's all right,'' she crooned, stroking her son's hair. ''It's just a nightmare, Danny.''

The child clung to her as if she were his only link to reality in a world of bloody fantasy. Matthew knew the feeling well. He found himself rocking slightly on his heels, matching the comforting rhythm she was using to soothe her child.

After a few moments, he began to feel uncomfortable, as if he were violating some sanctity that existed only between mother and child. Yet he felt compelled to watch. After a few more minutes, Jill seemed to have gotten control of the situation, her son snuggled peacefully in her arms.

"Uh...is there anything I can do?" he offered softly.

She looked up at him with a tear-streaked face that cut a neat path right to his gut. "You mentioned help. What kind of help?"

Matthew drew a deep breath. "I have a friend who is a child psychologist. He knows how to help in situations like this."

Jill's face tightened.

"Call him."

"I already have."

"THE GREATEST Show on Earth!"

That's what I'd exclaimed when I cornered my prey. The man whimpered for pity, for rescue, perhaps even for forgiveness. But when the knife hit its mark, no one had heard the roar of his greasepaint. And even though he screamed, his painted smile remained in place, ever cheerful, ever bright.

I'd looked down at his outfit, watching the blood drip down, playing connect the dots with the polka-dot material of his clown suit. That was the image that inspired this particular memory page.

I opened the scrapbook to that page which bulged a bit more than the others. Initially, I had hopes of getting a death mask, an imprint of his painted features to add to my collection of memorabilia. But he ruined that by smearing his makeup as he fell. Careless bastard.

His smudged eyes opened and he dared to ask "Why?" with his last dying breath. I decided at that moment that if knowledge was power, then this man would enter the gates of Hell powerless. I made sure he was dead before I allowed myself to answer his pitiful question.

"No child shall suffer ever again at your hands."

It was then that I realized that those offensive hands were hiding in garish-colored gloves. That would not do—it simply would not do. So I did the only thing I could, considering the circumstances—I stripped off his gloves and after a flash of brilliance, I sliced off each fabric fingertip, knowing that they would make a lovely addition to my book of memories.

And there they were, adding a bit of extra thickness that kept the pages from lining up exactly. But I tolerated its inconsistency.

As I stroked the slightly soiled cotton, a child's chant filled my ears.

"This little clown went to the circus."

"This little clown stayed home."

"This little clown...is dead."

Chapter Seven

"Hi, Danny. I'm Oskar. But I'm no grouch."

Dr. Oskar McGrath made no noise as he squatted down so that he was at eye level with the child, but the physical discomfort associated with the movement was evident in his face. "Your mom tells me you've had a rough time lately."

Danny said nothing, not even deigning to look in Oskar's direction. Instead, he paid inordinate attention to his army man.

Oskar leaned forward. "I heard that your daddy was killed and you were there when it happened."

Jill took an involuntary step forward, a protective gleam in her eyes. However, Matthew intercepted her by reaching for her hand. He shook his head. "Doc knows what he's doing," he whispered.

A tremor passed through her hand and she returned his grasp with her own tight one. He glanced over to the doorway where his friend, Jeff, Oskar's son, stood with his hands stuffed in his pockets, his brows knitted in concern. Jeff looked up and acknowledged Matthew's notice with a nod and soft sigh. "Poor kid," he mouthed.

Oskar continued, ignoring them all and speaking only to Danny. "That must have been awfully scary."

The child gave him one furtive glance before turning his attention back to the army man. He made a percussive noise with his mouth as he directed his soldier to shoot a torn-out magazine picture he'd propped up against a wooden bowl. With the easy flick of Danny's finger, the paper victim performed a spectacular swan dive off the edge of the coffee table.

"Got 'em," Danny growled.

Jill's grip on Matthew's hand tightened, growing almost painful.

Oskar reached down and retrieved the picture. "You think maybe you and I can spend a little time together?"

Danny shrugged, suddenly looking more like an old man than a four-year-old boy. "S'okay."

Oskar shifted so that he could sit on the couch next to Danny. He held the magazine cutout close to his face, peering at it intently.

Matthew stiffened; he knew Oskar had retired due to his failing eyesight, but he didn't know it had gotten quite this bad. He glanced at Jeff, who shared a tight-lipped smile.

Oskar continued. "So…are these the guys from *Toy Story*? Let's see this one in the picture has a bazooka and yours looks like the radio guy."

"Com-mu-ni-ca-tions officer," Danny corrected.

A smile lit Oskar's face. "I stand corrected." He turned to Matthew and Jill. "You two go away. Danny and I will be fine here. Right, Danny?"

The child shrugged again, but made no protests and no efforts to stop Jill as Matthew tugged at her hand, hoping to pull her out of the room. When she seemed unwilling to move, he leaned over and whispered, "C'mon. Doc knows what he's doing. God knows, he's done it before."

Jill looked into his eyes, her gaze burning a hole to his soul. "Before?"

All of the sudden, he wanted to tell her everything, share every fear, every moment of guilt, every thought of childish fright…the very things she had no business hearing at the moment. Instead, Matthew felt himself nodding and reducing his entire sordid explanation to two simple words.

"With me."

He waited until they got into the dining room before he surrendered to the wave of emotion that threatened him. Closing his eyes, he wondered if the demons from the past would break loose, released by his simple admission.

"With you," Jill repeated. "You mean…"

He swallowed back the bitter taste of bad memories and opened his eyes. "Dr. McGrath…Oskar worked with me, helped me learn how to deal with what I saw, what I knew. He's the one who first listened to me when I said I knew something about the man who killed my father. Oskar will reach Danny and help him find a way to cope, too."

They moved toward the kitchen where Jill lingered in the doorway, trying to keep an eye on her son in the living room.

"C'mon. You'll just be in the way," Matthew continued in a low voice.

"But I'm his mom…." It was a simple explanation, concise but meaningful. Her sigh spoke volumes as well.

"It'll be okay." Matthew managed a smile, but she

ignored it as she took a step toward the living room, wearing her disconsolation like an itchy sweater. Matthew glanced down and realized her fingers were firmly intertwined in his. It seemed perfectly natural for him to lift her hand to his lips and kiss the back of it lightly. "I promise."

To her credit, she didn't pull away, but she did tear her stare away from the living room and turn it toward him.

Heat rose from the collar of his shirt and a thousand regrets flew through his mind.

You don't know her.

She doesn't know you.

She's just been through a trauma.

This is no time to make any sort of—he swallowed hard—*romantic overtures.*

What the hell had gotten into him? He wasn't into chivalric gestures or anything like that. But it seemed so...simple, so appropriate for that moment in time and space.

But to his surprise, Jill's stare was neither blank nor hostile. Her look of shock contained something else—something personal. God help him, she looked as if given any other time and any other place, she might find his action...acceptable. Even welcome.

Then as quickly as the look flared in her eyes, it faded. She glanced toward the living room again. "He's really good? Dr. McGrath, that is?"

"Dad's the best."

Both of them flinched, making it evident neither had realized Jeff McGrath had followed them into the kitchen.

"If it weren't for his eyesight, Dad would still be

practicing. But all he does now is sit around the house, feeling useless.''

Matthew clapped his friend on the shoulder. ''I didn't realize how bad it had gotten. I talk to him all the time, but it's usually on the phone.''

Jeff shrugged. ''He wouldn't have mentioned it to you. Heck, he's practically blind now and damn near inconsolable. But this—'' Jeff nodded toward the living room ''—has to be the best thing to happen to him in years.'' He looked at Jill and colored quickly. ''I'm sorry. I didn't mean I think it's good that this happened to you and your son.'' He glared at Matthew as if to say, ''Help me!''

Jill managed a half smile. ''I understand what you mean. Your father no longer feels useless now that someone needs him. You don't know how much I appreciate having a trained professional willing to come here.'' She looked up and scanned Jeff's features. ''And thank you, too, for dropping everything and bringing him here so quickly.''

Jeff grinned. ''I like feeling useful, too. Anyway...'' He elbowed Matthew in the ribs. ''I'm glad to have an excuse to come. Matt's the brother I never had. It's been almost a year since we've seen each other, right, bud?''

Matthew felt a smile pull at his lips. ''Time flies. How's business?''

Jeff's grin broadened. ''Fantastic. The Internet has turned out to be a great place to conduct business. You don't need stationery, business cards, secretaries, anything. I don't even have drive to work anymore. Bringing Dad here is the first time my car's been out of the garage in a week.''

''I'm glad the venture's been a success.''

"Me, too. It was a gamble, but a good one." Jeff turned to Jill. "What business are you…?" His voice faded away. Although Jill was facing him, her gaze carried over his shoulder and into the living room. Matthew looked past Jeff as well and saw Oskar leaning over and whispering something in Danny's ear. Although Danny was covering his mouth, they could see the corners of his grin. He whispered something back to Oskar which made the old man burst out in laughter.

"See?" Matthew whispered. "They're getting along great."

Jill shook her head. "I've never seen Danny warm up like this with men before. First you and now Dr. McGrath."

"He may be looking for a male role model or father substitute, now that his real father is gone."

She crossed her arms. "He'd have to know what a real father was to begin with. Bummpt was no father to him. Just a man who intruded in his life at unexpected times and then forgot about him when it wasn't convenient." She turned around and pinned Matthew with a steely stare. "Do you really think it's wise to let him get attached to the doctor and to—" She stopped short before including Matthew. He found it an interesting omission, one he'd take time to contemplate later. But he couldn't help but notice the way she avoided his gaze.

She continued, pointedly directing her conversation to Jeff. "After all, I don't live here. As soon as the police agree to let us leave, we'll return home. I have a job and Danny has preschool."

Although unaware of some of the undercurrents of the conversation, Jeff offered his own analysis of the situation. ''It seems to me that if my father can unlock Danny's memories, and you're able to use that information to protect him from or even capture a murderer, then the potential problem of separation anxiety is inconsequential in comparison.''

Matthew watched her tempter begin to flare. ''You don't know—''

The phone rang, effectively cutting her off. Thankful for the interruption, Matthew shot her a quick apologetic smile, and reached around her to retrieve the phone, putting himself between her and Jeff.

''Hello?''

''It's me.'' Greg Solati continued without identifying himself as usual. ''Listen, something just came off the wire that you need to see.''

''I told you, Greg, I'm on leave of absence. I'm not coming in to work and you can't—''

''Would you shut up for a minute and listen? The police were in here earlier, asking questions about you. They told me your sister is still in the hospital. Sorry, man. Anyway, we're working on a story about Bummpt when something rang a bell. It's the same knife.''

''Same knife? I don't understand.''

''Remember the big story that you almost turned down because you were working on that stupid book of yours? The one about the stock car racers?''

''The McCreedy Boys? Vernon and...what's-his-name?''

''Billy. Vernon and Billy. Yeah, remember the big to-do the police made about the knife that was used on their car? Some oddball survivalist weapon? Well, turns out someone offed Bummpt with the same type of knife.''

Matthew's fingers tightened around the receiver. "A pattern..."

"Maybe. You want the story? Or are you too engrossed in the literary world to remember your roots as a reporter?"

The skin prickled on the back of Matthew's neck. Something inside of him was screaming "Take it!" but another side of him made him turn around and look at Jill, who had forgotten her moment of anger with Jeff and was mesmerized by the sight of her son and the doctor playing with the plastic soldier.

Greg barked in his ear. "The story has to be filed in two hours. If you can't do it, I got two or three guys here chomping at the bit."

"Yeah, I want it." Matthew drew a deep breath. "I'll be there in fifteen."

Greg released a sigh that smacked of relief. "Good. What do you need?"

"Start pulling the files on Bummpt. Standard background stuff. And pull the stuff on the McCreedys, too. And start a search for any other deaths by stabbing in the last...six months. Okay?"

"Gotcha."

"And Greg?"

"Yeah?"

"Good catch."

"You're welcome, kemosabe. It'll be good to have you back, even if only for a little while."

Matthew hung up the phone and turned to his companions. "I've got to go."

"What?" Jill turned her attention from her son to him, stepping closer. She paled. "Is it your sister?"

A pang of conscience shut down every electrified nerve in his body. For one glorious moment, he'd been alive with excitement and anticipation at the thought of delving into a cryptic puzzle. But Jill was able to bring him right back down to earth with two very well-chosen words, *your sister.*

He took a deep breath. "No, nothing about Carol. It's—it's another matter. I've got to go into the office. There's an…emergency that needs my attention. Are you going to be all right here? They've posted a cop outside to watch things."

Jeff took a step forward. "Listen, Dad and I have nothing pressing today. We can stay as long as I can use your computer to check my e-mail."

"That's fine with me…if it's okay with Jill." He faced her. "I won't be that long—two hours, three tops."

She shook her head. "Don't worry about us. We'll be fine." Giving him a critical glance, she lifted her hand and touched his cheek. "Be careful. We don't know who…or where or…"

"Don't worry about me." He reached down and picked up her hand, twining his fingers in hers. "I'll be fine. If you need anything, hit redial one and you'll get the office. Now, are you sure you're going to be okay?"

They stood there, inordinately close, hand in hand. The next logical step wasn't one of logic, rather of emotion, but neither of them seemed willing to take that step.

She answered only with a nod, hesitant at first, then resolute. Ducking her head, she turned away, pulling her hand from his. But graced with a view of the back of her head, he noticed a fine flush of color spreading up her neck.

How long had it been since he'd seen a woman

blush over something as innocuous as someone holding her hand?

How long had it been since holding a woman's hand had made his heart take an extra beat? Like now?

He made the mistake of glancing at Jeff who raised an eyebrow in silent response and made a grand show of looking at Jill and then back at Matthew.

"Smooth operator," Jeff mouthed.

It was the sort of smart-ass remark Jeff always made during their years as college buddies, but now, such flippancy seemed damned immature, considering the situation. He scowled at Jeff and grabbed his car keys from the counter.

As he strode toward the door, he felt Danny's stare burn a hole through him. Matthew suddenly remembered the suffocating sense of helplessness and the lack of control that marked the bloody days of his early youth. The least he could do was let the boy know what was going on. He pivoted at the door and gestured to Danny.

"Hey, sport, I got to go to my office. Will you keep an eye on your mom and the house for me? I'll be back in a couple of hours."

A dubious light flared in Danny's eyes. "Yeah... sure you will." He spoke the words with such frigidity that Matthew stopped and stared.

"What's wrong?"

Danny crossed his arms and stuck out his lips in stony silence, offering no explanation.

Matthew turned to Oskar, hoping for some explanation. *What did I say wrong?* he gestured. A split second later, Matthew realized he was probably no more than a hazy blur to Oskar's failing eyes. Empathy washed over him as he realized how limiting a sightless world must be to a man who spent so much of his career reading the body language, facial expressions and wordless gestures of his patients.

Would Oskar sense by other means the fat tear rolling down Danny's cheek or the look of disappointment that flared in the boy's eyes?

"At ease, soldier," Oskar commanded. He turned to Matthew. "Give me a minute."

Oskar pulled Danny into his arms and held a terse but quiet conversation with the child. Several moments later, Oskar straightened and directed an unfocused stare in Matthew's direction.

"It's a case of semantics, I'm afraid. It seems that Danny's dad used to call him sport and promise to return in a couple of hours. Then he would disappear for months."

Suddenly, Matthew could feel every fiber of the child's disappointment, confusion and hurt, not to mention the waves of anger flowing from Jill. Of course she'd been the one left to explain why Daddy didn't choose to come around any more.

Up to now, he'd concentrated on what he and Danny had in common, but now, he could see all the ways that their childhood differed. No matter what had happened, Matthew had always known that his father loved him without limits, without conditions and had not chosen to leave, but was taken against his will.

Danny didn't even have the security of his father's love to see him through this bloody mess.

Although the editorial clock was ticking away precious time, right now, Danny was more important than anything or anybody in the world. Matthew moved swiftly across the room to Danny's side and squatted down to face him. Danny shied away from him, taking refuge not in Oskar's grandfatherly embrace, but behind his plastic soldier.

"I promise I'll never lie to you like that Danny," Matthew whispered. "If I say a couple of hours, that's what I mean. If it's going to be longer, I'll tell you the truth."

Danny refused to look at him, paying inordinate attention to his toy soldier instead.

"And when I call you 'sport,' I do that because that's what my father used to call me. When he called me that, I knew that I was his very best buddy in the whole world and that he loved me. He never ever called anybody else that name but me. It meant he loved me."

Danny's lip trembled. "Then you love me?"

Tangled webs be damned. "In a way. A sort of 'we've just met but I know you're really special' way. Maybe *love* is too strong of a word to use yet. But I know that I like you a whole bunch. I care what happens to you...and your mom. And I promise to never called any other kid in the world 'sport,' but you."

His eyes opened wide. "Really?"

Matthew started to trace an *X* on his chest. "Cross my heart and hope—"

"No!" Danny reached out and stopped Matthew in midgesture. "Don't hope for that." He threw himself into Matthew's arms.

Matthew swallowed hard, remembering a similar situation years ago and the strength of Dr. Oskar McGrath's protective grasp in return. He ruffled the child's hair in very much the way his hair had been ruffled. "You're right, Danny," he whispered, "it's not the type of thing you should hope for." He pulled back, wiped away the child's tears and stuck out his hand. "I'll be back. Promise."

Danny accepted his hand and shook it solemnly. He paused then added, "You really like me a whole bunch?"

Matthew fought the urge to tear up himself. He grinned instead as he stood. "I really do. I really like you a whole big bunch."

Matthew pivoted, catching sight of Jill who quickly turned away. *And I like you a whole bunch, too.*

Chapter Eight

Although Matthew had only been away for five months on his writing sabbatical, he'd managed to forget the level of noise that filled the city room at this hour of the publishing day. Working at home, he'd grown use to composing his thoughts in peace and quiet, interrupted only occasionally by Mrs. Flynn and her vacuum cleaner. But now, he had to struggle to reclaim his ability to concentrate in the middle of bedlam.

He slid into his usual seat, still warm from the reporter who'd occupied it only moments before. Studying the monitor, he realized Greg Solati had done his usual good job of combing through the files and collecting all pertinent background details, not to mention pulling up Matthew's own notes which were buried in the computer archives.

He began to read the articles.

The Thunder Rolls No More
by Matthew Childs, Feature Reporter
Tragedy struck the racing world today when brothers, Vernon "Thunder" and Billy "Lightning" McCreedy died while taking their practice

laps in preparation for the Carlston 500 at Carlston International Raceway. Witnesses reported that Vernon lost control in the first turn and his Grand Prix exploded on impact when it hit the wall. Billy attempted to steer around the fireball, but he also lost control and momentum sent him over the wall. According to officials, Billy McCreedy died while en route to the Carlston hospital....

Did Lightning Strike Twice?
by Matthew Childs, Feature Reporter

Track officials, the McCreedy pit crew and Carlston police are working together to either substantiate or dispel rumors that the McCreedy brothers died as a result of sabotage. Only hours after the wrecked cars were towed to the McCreedy garage, the pit crew discovered several suspicious mechanical anomalies during their automotive autopsies. The police are not commenting at this time, but speculation runs rampant about suspicious cuts in fuel lines, brake lines and steering linkages.

Thunder and Lightning Felled by Sabotage
by Matthew Childs, Feature Reporter

In a trackside press meeting, Carlston track officials and the police shocked the racing community by announcing that the official cause of death for Vernon and Billy McCreedy was death by a person or persons unknown. Automotive experts examined the remains of both cars and confirmed speculations that the brothers were victims of deliberate sabotage.

According to the experts, someone tampered with the throttle of Vernon McCreedy's black Grand Prix, causing it to stick as he was going into the first turn. His brakes failed, due to a brake line interruption, which caused him to lose control and slam into the wall at over a hundred miles per hour. His brother, Billy, lost control while attempting to steer around Vernon's flaming wreckage. Officials say someone tampered with both the brakes and the steering linkage of his silver 1997 Grand Prix as well. Police have named no suspects but they are reportedly investigating Carlston track personnel, members of the joint McCreedy pit crew, and several unnamed fellow racers.

Last year, Vernon McCreedy was involved in a highly publicized paternity suit which propelled him into some unflattering limelight, but the brothers' first-second place finishing in the Barnyard 500 turned the spotlight elsewhere.

Subsequent articles written after Matthew went on sabbatical added no new details. But he knew an aspect of the case that the general public hadn't been told. As a professional courtesy to Sid and an honest desire to see the saboteur caught, Matthew deliberately left out a description of the odd knife markings on the severed lines. It had only been happenstance that he'd seen the actual brake line up close—close enough to see the rippled cut made by a knife with a serrated blade.

A quick call to the tools expert at the state forensic lab had told him what he needed to know; a blade like that could be identified, distinguished from other knifes, even of the same make and model by the series of scratches and nicks on the blade. Their classification system worked similar to the way a ballistics test could identify and classify a bullet as coming from a specific gun.

This revelation grew more important in light of the large assortment of implements readily at hand in a garage. Any of them could have been used to sever the various lines and linkages, but after testing, the forensics team announced that none of the various blades, knives, screwdrivers, wire cutters, or tin snips left the same dimpled cut. That meant the saboteur had brought his own weapon of choice, which substantiated the theory of premeditation.

And something even more important: the killer might still have the murder weapon.

Of course, soon after the McCreedy brothers' crash, another racer blamed his race loss on a similar claim of sabotage, using the opportunity to milk his lucky survival for publicity's sake. The police quickly discounted his claims due to the clumsy trail of clues that led back to himself as chief culprit. Lucky for him, the offending tire had been slashed with a straight-edged knife or he might have been hauled in as a possible suspect in the McCreedy deaths.

But now the same oddly dimpled pattern of serration had surfaced again.

Someone used the same style knife to kill Daniel McFadden.

And tried to kill Carol. Don't forget about Carol.

Matthew pushed away the mental image of his sister fighting for her life and tried to concentrate on the stark words on the computer screen. The best way to help her was to help unravel this mystery. She'd never wanted his sympathy or his involvement in her world, before or now.

But she called you, echoed a persistent voice in the back of his head. *She could have called 911. She* should *have called 911, but she called you, instead.*

He pushed away the annoying echoes of conscience and turned his attention to the other files on his screen.

Two similarities didn't make a pattern. Geometrically speaking, two points only formed a line. What he needed was a third point in hopes of forming some sort of shape.

The shape of murder…

He looked at every article printed in his paper in the past two years that mentioned a death or attack that mentioned a knife either as a murder weapon or involved in any aspect of the death. He waded through reports of gang killings, attacks by jealous lovers, school yard altercations…anything where a knife had been utilized, directly or indirectly.

A few odd cases started to surface from the usual reports of mayhem that filled the electronic morgue. One in particular stood out. He glanced at his own name in the byline and the facts flooded his mind.

Eight months ago, the president of a large medical supply warehouse had committed suicide by carbon monoxide poisoning. Matthew remembered the case well. Nelson Chandler had simply risen from his king-size bed one day, dressed in his usual business attire—a charcoal gray suit, white oxford shirt, red power tie—wrote a farewell note to his family vacationing in Aspen, and then went to his four-car garage. There, he stepped past his Mercedes, his Range Rover, the empty spot where his wife's Jag usually sat, and stopped at his cherished, vintage '65 Mustang. Then he used a piece of ordinary garden hose to reroute the exhaust from the tailpipe to the triangular vent window on the driver's side of the car.

Then he climbed in behind the steering wheel....

And waited.

Evidently, the car ran undisturbed for several hours before neighbors grew suspicious of the noise and the clouds of exhaust seeping from beneath the garage door.

At the time of discovery, the police noted that the garden hose had been cut a specific length for the task from a larger section of hose sitting on a tool bench, also inside the garage. Chandler had painstakingly used duct tape to neatly hold the hose in place on the tailpipe and sealing the window opening with his usual precision. The only clue that pointed in any direction other than suicide was the fact that no one could find the oddly serrated knife which had been used to slice through the plastic garden hose. However the police explained the absence by deciding he'd been planning his death for some time and could have prepared the hose in advance and disposed of the knife days, even weeks earlier.

But what had merely been a moment of inconsistency now glared like a neon sign to Matthew.

An oddly serrated knife.

Was the knife the key that strung these seemingly random crimes together? But the knife would have nothing to do with how they were selected, would it? What did these people have in common?

Matthew pulled out a legal pad and began to doodle, his usual way of organizing his thoughts. Three dots formed a triangle, each one representing a victim—

Bummpt, the McCreedy Brothers as a single entity and Nelson Chandler. What did they have in common?

They were all male.

Of course, if Carol was supposed to be a victim as well as or in lieu of Bummpt, then that pattern was broken. However, considering the level of controversy Bummpt had created over the span of his career, Carol was most likely an innocent bystander in Matthew's uneducated opinion. At least he would take that particular approach in this exercise in deduction; to consider her as an intended target became almost paralyzing. *Like father, like daughter?* Never.

He dragged his attention back to the notepad.

All male. What else? Bummpt lived in a nice middle-class residential neighborhood, which was almost anticlimactic, considering how much money he supposedly made as "The Man America Loves to Hate." Maybe those FCC fines added up after a while.

The McCreedys called home a place in Alabama— a town called Montevallo. It sounded lush, green and small. When they raced at various tracks around the country such as the Carlston, they stayed in a tour bus that rivaled anything owned by the top country-and-western stars.

Chandler lived in a high-class community where most of the houses bordered a private golf course. Whereas most people attempting suicide merely waited for their garages to fill with exhaust fumes, Chandler's garage was spacious enough to hold four cars. He must have realized how long it would take to fill the large area with enough deadly gas to kill himself, thus he came up with the hose contraption that easily filled the small interior airspace of the car.

Okay, that meant there was no obvious correlation

between the size of town they lived, in the location or the type of neighborhood.

Matthew drew doodles to represent interests and hobbies.

Golf? Chandler was the only duffer in the group.

Tennis? Only Bummpt played.

Women?

According to the paper's radio columnist, Bummpt played the field—at least his radio persona talked non-stop about his nocturnal conquests. The sports department confirmed that the McCreedys were legendary Lotharios. However, Chandler was a choirboy, a dedicated husband of thirty-two years who left a grieving family behind.

Vices?

All four men drank, but none reportedly to excess. Bummpt reportedly steered away from smoking to safeguard his voice and therefore his career. However, the entertainment editor offered an interesting anecdote about a gift box of exploding cigars. Too bad they had only been gag gifts.

The McCreedys had one minor run-in with the law during their juvie days concerning a couple of joints, a pint of Jack Daniel's and an illegal drag race. But the race commission always kept its drivers under rigorous testing and the McCreedys had tested clean for over three years.

The only connection at all with Chandler was the fact that his medical supply company probably provided the drug test kits for the racers.

"Drug tests." Matthew said the words aloud as if to test the validity of the concept.

Did disc jockeys have to take drug tests?

"Oh great." Greg Solati propelled his office chair

toward Matthew and brazenly stared over his shoulder at the legal pad. "So this is you're idea of a lead story? An artistic interpretation of crime in the twentieth century?" He shook his head and clucked his tongue. "You'll never make it as an editorial cartoonist."

"Leave me alone." Matthew tapped his pencil against the paper, making a series of random dots. "I'm thinking."

"You should be writing." Greg stared at the paper and then at Matthew for an inordinately long time. Finally, he drew a deep breath and released it as an exasperated whistle between his teeth. "I've lost you, haven't I?" He leaned back in his chair and groaned. "God I hate it when reporters decide to become writers. B.S.—'Before Sabbatical'—you'd hash me out a story, a good one and on time, too. But now, all you want to do is stew in your creative juices. Damn it!"

Greg pushed off from Matthew's desk, shot his chair across the corridor and yelled at the nearest reporter, "The Bummpt case. Give me six column inches in twenty minutes. Updates are filed under Childs' directory, Bum-004."

The recipient of the orders groaned, but bent over his computer to fit the facts together in a suitable journalistic jigsaw.

But Matthew knew he had a bigger puzzle to solve. "Greg, drugs and radio stations. What's the correlation?"

Greg screwed up his face. "There was a case last year with a morning drive-time guy who had a hard time getting his energy up in the early a.m. He turned to the wonders of modern prescription medicines. One morning, he took one too many uppers and finished his four-hour broadcast in about an hour forty-five. The station wasn't happy. Neither were the sponsors.''

Matthew's mind leapt to the next conclusion. "Let me guess. They ended up instituting some sort of drug test for their deejays."

Greg shook his head. "Nah...nothing like that. They footed the bill for rehab, gave him another chance, but ended up firing him three months later. Wait..." His brows furrowed. "You think Bummpt may have had a monkey on his back?"

Matthew shrugged. "I don't know. You heard any rumors headed in that direction?"

Greg shook his head again. "Nary a one. But why don't you call his producer?" He closed his eyes and plumbed his magnificently deep and sometimes unbelievable datasink called his brain. "Crenshaw. Leggy, icy, surly...L-I-S..." He snapped his fingers. "Lisa. Lisa Crenshaw. Ms. Hardball 1998."

Matthew remembered Danny's statement about how his father and Ms. Crenshaw were "adult fighting." If there was no love lost between the two, then maybe she would be willing to answer some questions, no matter if they posthumously stained an already tarnished reputation

He used Greg's private office for the call, not wanting to broadcast the unmistakable fact that he was sitting in the middle of a city room in full swing. Plus if she was as hard-nosed as her reputation suggested, she'd probably run caller ID on every call and have all the standard press numbers memorized. Greg prided himself on making sure his private line didn't show up on any of the media databases.

But getting to Lisa Crenshaw wasn't easy. Matthew fought his way through a couple of fire-wall secretaries, several sulky interns and two rude production assistants before getting her on the phone. God forgive him, but he used his relationship with Carol as his calling card. It was one thing to answer questions from Joe Q. Person, private citizen, and another to make a statement for a member of the press.

"Ms. Crenshaw? I hope this isn't a bad time to talk. I'm Carol McFadden's brother."

She sounded as if no time was a good time to talk, but knew she had to be somewhat sympathetic. "I'm sorry about your sister," she said curtly. "How is she?"

"Better," he lied, his stomach twisting in a guilty knot. He had no idea if Carol was better or not. "I was calling to ask you a couple questions about my brother-in-law Daniel...er...Bummpt..." He hesitated, then added in a sort of aw-shucks way, "I really didn't know him that well and I was...wondering if he might have had some dealings with a...rougher element." He let some of his real frustration slip to the surface.

She sniffed in distaste. "By rougher elements, you mean...what?"

He knew not to play the ace up front. "I'm not sure. Maybe loan sharks. You know...gambling debts. I've heard him on the radio more than once, talking about how he'd slept with lots of women. Maybe a jealous husband decided to take revenge." He lowered his voice. "Or maybe it had something to do with drugs. You know what they say about...entertainers. Could it have been a drug deal gone bad?"

She covered the mouthpiece, but Matthew could hear her ordering someone to get her car. She returned to the phone. "Sorry. How should I put this?" She hesitated for a moment, which turned out to be more of a dramatic pause. "Bummpt squeezed every dollar he made until George Washington had that pyramid stuck up his butt." Her laugh was unattractive. "I can promise you that Bummpt liked money way too much to gamble with it. And as to drugs, I may have hated that sonovabitch, but I'll have to admit, he always stayed clean. He'd never messed with any hard stuff for as long as I'd known him...which was too damn long for my likes." She paused, then asked in a stiffer voice as if she realized what she'd admitted to a total stranger. "What did you say your name was?"

Matthew knew the gears were starting to turn. "Matthew, Carol McFadden's brother."

"Matthew...Carol..."

He could hear her flipping through some paper.

A sudden chill filled the air. "Carol's maiden name was Childs? You're Matthew Childs?" She almost growled. "From the *Times*?"

He heard something large crash. A paperweight? A lamp? The entire desk?

She erupted in a flow of expletives. "Damn it, Childs, this was off the record. If you quote me in that rag of yours, I'll—"

"Don't worry. It's off the record, Ms. Crenshaw. I'm not calling on behalf of the paper. I'm only calling for me—for personal reasons."

"Well, I'd say you're about six years too late with your brotherly concern," she sneered. Then she began to mimic him in a falsetto. "Was he a gambler? Did he drink? Did he piss off his drug dealer?" Her tone lowered to its normal register. "Where were all these questions and all this loving protection when your sister ran off and married that chauvinistic blowhard? Where were you?''

Lisa Crenshaw banged the receiver down so hard that Matthew jumped.

Where in hell *had* he been? And what in the hell was he going to do about it now?

"It's a matter of trust," Oskar said, between tentative sips of coffee. "I need to build Danny's trust in me. Tell me, does he interact with either of his grandfathers?"

Jill glanced across the room at her son who was quite content at the moment, kneeling by the coffee table, building a house of cards. "He doesn't have one. My father died several years ago, before he was born. And if Bummpt had a father, he lost track of him years ago. I've never met any of Bummpt's family."

Oskar nodded. "It's easier to believe men like him were hatched, rather than born of woman." A harsh look filled his hazy eyes then passed as quickly as it formed. "I'm sorry, dear. He was your husband for a while, wasn't he?"

For one brief moment, she wanted to say something in support of Bummpt, but she could find little to say to his credit. Too many things had been blurring her judgment when Bummpt came into her life—booze, lust, an irresponsible lifestyle. It was as if she woke up one day and discovered him in bed and realized who and what she'd married. Even now, she found it hard to believe she'd attempted to love a man whose only real redeemable feature and benefit to the world at large had been his genetic donation to their son. For

Danny's sake, couldn't she find something positive to say about his father?

She glanced at her son. "Danny's the only good thing that came out of my marriage. Hard to believe someone so sweet and loving could have sprung from someone so offensive."

Oskar shook his head. "Don't be so harsh on yourself. Sometimes, marriage ends up forging a relationship between two disparate people and both become better people for it. But there are those marriages in which only one person grows stronger. Like steel, you hardened when exposed to high heat and you developed enough strength to leave and take Danny with you. I admire that in a woman, in any person caught in an unsavory situation."

Was she supposed to thank him for pointing out the obvious but painful truth? She didn't need anybody to tell her how stupid, how naive she'd been to get involved with someone like Bummpt. And she certainly didn't need the absolution of a perfect stranger to forgive her sins.

Oskar needed to remember he was there to help Danny, not—

"But I realize you don't need an old man to tell you all this." A truly warm smile crossed his face. "Danny is our concern right now."

She forgot her criticisms, finding herself quite willing to forgo them if it meant helping her son. "How is he?"

Oskar lifted one shoulder. "Confused. Like most children his age, he doesn't have a good grasp on the finality of death. Every once in a while as we talk, he asks me if his father will come back some day."

"What did you tell him?"

Oskar toiled over his coffee, almost as if he were stalling. "I believe in telling the truth, especially when a question is couched in a manner like his. Danny wants someone to tell him the truth, even if that truth is a painful one to accept." He looked up over his mug. "Once he accepts the truth, then he'll need to talk about his father's death and to work out his own concept of death as a departure from life."

"But he's only four."

"And how many characters has a four-year-old child watched die on television, only to see them resurrected the next week in a new role or a rerun? Danny's heard the concept of death bandied about for some time, but his only experience with it is theatrical. Nothing but false blood or gentle passings into the night." Oskar's voice grew taut. "But that's not what he saw. Your son saw death at its most violent and bloodiest and he has to purge it from his soul."

"You sound like Matthew."

"No, Matthew sounds like me. He's picked up some of his philosophy from me, as well as some of my terminology over the years. The trouble is, we have to rush the timetable with Danny. I'm usually a proponent of letting the child tell his story when he's ready to tell it, but if your son is a witness to an unsolved murder and in danger, then we don't have the luxury of working by his internal time clock. Our job becomes a matter of helping him find a more expedient, yet healthy way to tell his story. Quite frankly, your son will not be safe until the police know what and who he saw."

Jill stared at him, not knowing whether she should run away from the man or throw her arms around him.

He spoke a bitter truth; their world had been turned upside down and no amount of wishing or hoping from her could change the sequence of past events. Danny had seen something or someone—his father's death or the man responsible for it, and their lives wouldn't be the same until the murderer was caught.

She glanced at her son, who had coerced Jeff to join him on the floor and help design a more elaborate house of cards. Jeff had folded his lanky figure in an uncomfortable position, but he seemed truly happy to be entertaining her son. At that moment, everything looked peaceful, normal. If allowed, she'd convince herself that everything *was* normal.

But it wasn't.

As Danny looked away, Jeff pulled out one of the load-bearing cards, causing the tower to tumble. When Danny turned back, startled by the collapse, Jeff grinned and taunted him with the card, just like one child playing with another. Her son stared at the destruction and then at the missing card, still held between Jeff's fingers. Reaching up, Danny calmly plucked free the card and tore it in half. He wore no expression—no anger, no disappointment, no guilt as he slowly tore the two pieces into four and then eight.

She stepped toward him, not willing to have his destructive behavior go unpunished, at least not without some sort of admonishment from her. But Oskar reached out, stopping her.

"Don't stop him. It's imperative that he knows it's all right to express himself."

Danny finished with one card and turned to the next.

As he tore the second card, his face changed and anger began to fill him. By the time he reached for the third card, he was in a rage.

Jeff glanced at his father, wearing a bewildered expression.

Oskar shook his head and motioned for the man to step back.

A shower of cards filled the air as Danny's anger mounted and he knocked over the coffee table.

Jill couldn't help herself; tantrums weren't her son's usual style. "Danny, stop!"

He stood still, his clenched hands at his sides, the cards settling into uneven piles at his feet. His shoulders heaved as he breathed, as he gasped for air.

"It's okay to be mad, but not to tear things up," she admonished.

His gasp grew more strained, his attempts to breathe more ragged. Belatedly realizing his action wasn't merely the manifestation of anger, Jill tore out of Oskar's grasp and almost vaulted the couch to reach Danny. He was choking, struggling for air, his face turning red.

"Danny, calm down. Everything's all right. Just breathe easily!" She pulled him into her arms and held him close.

His face continued to darken and he began to struggle weakly against her.

Jeff crossed his arms. "Aw he's okay...he's just holding his breath. Kids do that, right, Dad?"

Still clutching his half-full coffee mug, Oskar sloshed and stumbled through the maze of unfamiliar furniture and obstacles, and found his way to them. He moved beside her squinting to use what little eyesight he had left to examine Danny. "Did he aspirate a piece of a playing card?"

She managed to examine her son's mouth, despite his flailing and clawing of the air. "I can't see anything." She braced her son's small head between her palms, forcing him face her. "Danny, look at me. I want you to calm down. I want you to breathe slowly. In, two, three, four. Out, two, three, four."

Danny started to respond, but his attempts to inhale were nothing more than harsh wheezes.

Oskar cocked an ear. "Sounds like asthma." He turned around and barked his son's name.

Jeff held out his hands like a guilty child. "Don't look at me. I didn't do anything."

"I didn't say you did. Get me a half glass of water. Now!"

"But—"

"Now!" the doctor thundered. Jeff scurried off, returning moments later with the glass as ordered. Oskar poured the contents of his coffee into the water and held it out to Jill. "Get him to drink this."

"But—"

He braced a hand on her shoulder and lowered himself gingerly to his knees beside her. "Jill, just trust me. It'll help. But we also need to get him to a doctor."

As Jill helped her son sip the watered-down coffee, Oskar stood and turned in the general direction of his son. "Jeff, get the car. We have to take Danny to the hospital. Good Shepherd isn't that far from here and they have an excellent reputation for pediatric emergencies."

Jeff wore a look of momentary shock. "But I can't...I mean..."

"Now, Jeffrey!"

Jeff suddenly straightened, doubt fading from his face. "Of course, Father." He stuffed his hand in his pocket and pulled out a set of keys.

MATTHEW STARED at his drawing creating his little doodles and striking them off as no patten emerged between the three men beyond the knife. But maybe the knife was enough to bring to the attention of the police. He glanced at his watch. One quick call to Sid Morrison to explain his theories and then he'd head back home, placating Danny's fears of abandonment.

He rested his hand on the receiver and paused.

This must be what it feels like to have a child at the center of your universe. His thoughts wandered to Jill. What would it feel like to have a woman at the center of your being as well? Someone to share everything with—the fears, the cheers, the loneliness, the moments of exaltation.

Of course, the trick was to create those exalting moments together. He suddenly flashed on an image of her in his bed, twisted in his sheets, her head thrown back, her delicate neck exposed and ready to be kissed. He wasn't sure whether the look he was imagining on her face was exhilaration or laughter. Maybe they were one in the same.

He felt his body start to respond to his own thoughts. Maybe—

The phone at his desk rang and he picked it up.

"City Desk, Childs," he said, falling back into easy habit.

Oskar's usually controlled voice was rough, his words hurried. "Matthew...it's Danny. We're taking him to Good Shepherd Hospital. Meet us there."

Chapter Nine

Matthew slid into a parking place, stopping less than an inch from the bumper of the car opposite him. He took the concrete stairs from the parking lot to the hospital two at a time. Shouldering open the emergency room doors, he stumbled into a teeming mass of broken humanity awaiting treatment. Men, women, children filled the rows of faded plastic chairs. A muted television flickered in an upper corner of the waiting area.

Matthew scanned the sea of pale faces, looking for Jill and Danny, but they were nowhere to be seen.

Someone cleared their throat behind him. "Excuse me."

Matthew pivoted to face a woman in a pale blue uniform. She hugged her metal clipboard to her chest as if she needed a barrier to keep any patient from penetrating her outer defenses. Considering some of the more unsavory-looking patients awaiting treatment, it was a good idea to wear as much armor as possible.

She looked at him over a pair of half-frame glasses. "Can I help you, sir?"

"I'm looking for Jill and Danny McFadden. I got a

call at the office that Danny had been brought here. I don't know why." When she released the death grip on her chart, he strained to look at the papers clipped to it. Was that top page a list of admitted patients?

She consulted the clipboard. "Hmm…McFadden… yes, here it is." Her expression changed. "That's odd. He's already been admitted to Peds." She squinted at him over the clipboard with sudden respect. Her thoughts were plastered plainly on her face. *You must know someone high up who works here.*

Matthew glanced around at the confusing maze of signs that pointed to various areas of the hospitals. "Where's the Peds ward?"

The woman nodded at a pair of double doors. "Through there, turn right, through the next set of doors, then take the elevator to the fourth floor and check with the nurses' station." She graced him with a sweet smile, befitting someone who just might know someone high up. "Don't worry, Mr. McFadden. Your son is going to be fine."

It wasn't until Matthew was stepping out of the elevator on the fourth floor that he realized he'd made no effort to correct the nurse. She thought he was Danny's father. If that's what it took to get unrestricted access to the boy, then so be it.

He stopped at the nurses' station as directed and the young man behind the counter gave him Danny's room number. As Matthew trotted down the hallway, he realized that someone was standing guard at the doorway to Danny's room.

Someone in uniform.

His pulse quickened and he sped up. Had someone broken into the house? Did Bummpt's killer come back in hopes of silencing his only witness? Matthew's heart began to wedge itself into his throat, creating an uncomfortable lump.

Please let Danny be all right....

His gaze locked with that of the policeman who gave him a scathing once-over, obviously analyzing him for any potential of danger. The man's hand shifted nonchalantly down to his waist, toward his holstered gun.

From his experiences as a crime reporter, Matthew knew panic was an insidious emotion that could make an innocent man look guilty, a smart man look stupid and worst of all, a harmless man look threatening.

Matthew drew a deep breath, willing himself to swallow the flicker of panic. He didn't have time to waste pacifying a curious patrolman, no matter how glad he was to see someone guarding Danny's door.

The policeman's posture changed, adding at least an inch to his already impressive height. "May I help you?" he asked, forgoing the usually deferential, "sir." The underlying message was plain: If you don't belong, then you better get the hell out of here.

Matthew drew himself to his full height as well, unfortunately falling a couple inches shorter than the man. "My name is Matthew Childs. I'm here to see Danny McFadden."

"ID, please." The man scowled at him, his fingers grazing the butt of the gun at his side. "Slowly."

Matthew reached into his back pocket with an even, deliberate movement and gingerly extracted his wallet. It fell open to reveal his driver's license...and his press credentials.

The policeman flexed his shoulders, revealing an additional layer of steroid-enhanced muscle to his substantial bulk. He shifted in front of the door and crossed his arms, signifying that he'd categorized Matthew as a nuisance rather than a threat. "No press," he growled. "Beat it."

Matthew flipped his wallet shut. "I'm not here as a reporter. I'm here because—" a convenient excuse leapt to mind "—I'm Danny's uncle. At least, he thinks...er...he considers me his uncle."

The cop sneered. "Yeah, and I'm his third cousin, twice removed. Beat it, hack. If there's a press conference, they'll call you."

Matthew plowed a hand through his hair. "You don't understand. Danny's stepmother is my sister and—"

The policeman flexed again, then crossed his bulging arms to tap his fingers lightly on the radio mike clipped to his shirt pocket. He issued no threats, made no overt demonstrations of physical strength. Of course, he needed little else to be physically imposing other than his steely stance and stony stare. Matthew realized he'd received his one and only warning. The man would likely radio for backup and then calmly take Matthew out with one punch, maybe two if he managed to dodge the first.

Preferring an unblemished survival rather than unnecessary heroics, Matthew took a voluntary step backward, held out his palms in a classic I-have-nothing-to-hide gesture and raised his voice a notch. "Jill," he called to the door, "if you're in there, please come out and identify me. Jill?"

The policeman uncrossed his arms and rested his hand on the butt of his billy club. He'd probably been told guns made too much noise in the hospital corridors. "Listen mister, have some feelings for the kid.

He doesn't need to be disturbed. Go find some other news story, okay?''

The door cracked open and someone stared at them from the darkness within. Jill's voice emerged as a hoarse whisper. ''You're both disturbing him.''

He took advantage of the situation and stepped closer. ''Jill, is Danny okay? They wouldn't tell me—''

A meaty hand splayed across his chest and an inordinately soft voice purred in his ear. ''Listen, buster. I told you—''

''Stop.'' Jill leaned out to view the proceedings in the hallway. The guard paused with Matthew's shirt just beginning to pleat between his clenched fingers. Jill heaved a sigh. ''It's okay. He can come in.''

The policeman failed to remove his hand. ''But ma'am, he's a...a reporter.'' He made the word *reporter* sound just as charming as the word *rapist*.

Jill drew a deep breath. ''No, he's here because he's Danny's...uncle.'' Her hesitation before saying the word *uncle* made something in Matthew's chest twist. Before he could say anything to her, she disappeared back into the shadows of the room.

The policeman contemplated the revelation for a moment, then reluctantly pulled back his hand, pausing for a moment to give Matthew's collar a tweak of pseudoapologetic adjustment. Then he stepped aside, allowing Matthew to enter the dark doorway.

Entering the room, the first thing he noticed were the ominous-looking figures hovering around him. Matthew tensed his muscles in sheer reflex. As his eyes adjusted to the dim light, he realized that the looming shadows on the wall were merely cartoon figures in two-dimensional repose. If he was a kid, he'd sure hate to wake up in a strange room and a strange bed, only to see a hulking bear painted on the wall, even if it did wear a jaunty green hat and carry a picnic basket.

In the large rail-lined bed, Danny made a pitifully small lump under the thin covers. He looked pale, but comfortable, yet Matthew couldn't tear his gaze from the boy's face.

"He looks…okay. What happened?" he whispered to Jill, whom he sensed was sitting beside the bed, her elbows propped on the rail.

She reached over and brushed a lock of her son's hair off of his forehead. "He had an asthma attack."

Relief flooded through Matthew, unknotting muscles he didn't even know were tensed.

Asthma.

Not an attack by an unknown assailant. Not an emotional breakdown. Not a host of other outrageous injuries that had filtered through his mind as he drove to the hospital at speeds that should have gotten him arrested.

Matthew studied the boy carefully. Judging by his even rhythm of breath and his good color, Danny had survived his bout with asthma fairly unscathed. Matthew turned his critical gaze to from son to mother. But if Danny was all right, then why did Jill look so…upset?

He reached out for her. "Jill? Everything's okay, isn't it? I mean…Danny looks fine."

She nodded. "He is, now. It's just that…he'd never had a problem with asthma before." A tremor entered her voice. "Luckily, Oskar knew exactly what was happening and knew what to do to help." She swallowed hard. "But I'd never seen anybody have an asthma attack before." She leaned back from the bed and wrapped her arms around herself, looking almost as small and forelorn as Danny. "I felt so helpless," she whispered, "watching my baby gasp for breath. He turned red and then…"

Matthew wasn't sure who moved first, whether he reached for her or she reached him. All he knew was that they were standing at the foot of the bed, his arms were around her and she was sobbing into his shoulder.

Squeezing the words out between sobs, she managed to ask, "What kind of lousy mom lets this stuff happen to a sweet little boy like my Danny?"

Matthew instinctively tightened his arms around her, telling himself it was the proper thing to do when one human was comforting another. But what he felt wasn't the sympathy of comforting a fellow human being. What he was feeling was something stronger, more complicated, something almost thrilling.

Almost?

It *was* thrilling. He was thrilled to hold her, to have her pressed next to him, thrilled to realize she was finding momentary solace with him. And as suddenly as the thoughts filled him, he rejected them. What sort of creep takes advantage of a grieving woman? She needed compassion, not passion, in her life right now. At a time like this, the two just didn't mix, no matter how attracted he was to Jill, to her mind, her face, her body.…

She sobbed harder and he felt her tears dampen his shirt.

"It's okay," he crooned, using the same sort of voice he'd used to comfort Danny when they waited so many long hours for his mother to arrive. But there was a big difference between comforting a little boy and a grown woman.

A world of difference.

"I'm okay," she said, muffled in his shoulder. "Really."

He brushed a lock of hair off her forehead with the same gentle gesture she'd used for her son. "I know you are. But sometimes it helps to just let go. You're fine." He glanced at her son again. "And so is Danny. Look."

She wiped her eyes on the back of her hand, then stared at her son, peacefully sleeping in the hospital bed. To their collective surprise, the child roused, gave them a sleepy smile and reached out, patting the bed in search of a missing Mr. Popster.

"Momma...?" It was more of a complaint than an identification.

"Danny..." Jill released Matthew and scooted around the end of the bed to return to her son's side. "Shh, sweetheart, it's okay."

Matthew spotted the errant toy and squatted down, retrieving it from its hiding place between the mattress and the guardrails. "Here, sport."

Danny's smile flared again. "Thanks, Uncle Matt." Cuddling his toy, his eyes closed and he released a sleepy sigh. "I love you, Uncle Matt."

"I love you, too, Danny."

It was reflex—it had to be. It was something which seemed right at that moment as the words spilled free without effort. Even after he spoke, the words, the sentiments they held still seemed...appropriate. True, even. How could you not fall for a kid like him?

When Matthew turned around, Jill had taken several steps away. She stood in the darkness with her arms wrapped around herself again. He moved closer, in hopes that she'd find solace again in his arms, but instead of reaching for him, she sidestepped him.

"What's wrong?" he asked gently.

She said nothing.

"Jill?"

"It's not right," she whispered. "It's just not right." A note of hysteria crept into her soft voice.

He knew not to step any closer. She needed to define her space, not him. "What's not right?"

She unclenched her arms and lifted one hand, swiping her sleeve across her eyes. "*He* never said that. *He* never said 'I love you.'"

"Who? Danny?" He glanced at the child curled in the bed, a child who obviously loved his mother. Certainly Danny had said those words to Jill. As far as that went, hadn't Matthew actually heard Danny tell his mother he loved her, at least once?

"Not Danny, silly." She managed a small watery smile. "He's one of the most loving children you'll ever meet." The smile faded away into a scowl. "I mean Bummpt." She said his name as if it left a bad taste in her mouth. "He never once told Danny that he loved him. At least not that I know of."

Matthew thought back to his own father. It was almost comical to actually describe his dad, a printer, as a man of few words. Words were his life, speaking on a professional level. However, when it came to his family life, his father wasn't particularly verbal when it came to talking about love. But his actions always said volumes. Matthew may have not heard the actual words, *I love you* frequently from his father, but he knew, in no uncertain terms, that he was well loved.

An image of his father's proud smile swam through

his mind. "You know...some people find it hard to express sentiments like that aloud." He stopped suddenly. God help him, he was actually trying to defend that bastard, Bummpt.

Jill shook her head. "Not Bummpt. He never had a problem saying exactly what was on his mind. That's why he held the record for most FCC fines for obscene or lewd language on the radio." She leaned over the railing and tucked the blanket around her son. "A child can sense when someone loves him." Her loving gaze settled on her son and something wonderful lit her eyes.

Just like I can see the love a mother has for her son.

Her smile of maternal pride faded. "Danny always fought when it was time to visit his father." She sighed and sat down in the bedside chair. "I tried to make myself believe it was because of the divorce. But I know it was because Danny knew how his father felt about him." She paused. "Father," she muttered. "He was no more Danny's father than...than..." She dipped her head, a curtain of hair hiding her features. In the shadows, he could swear he saw her tremble.

There was a moment of silence, filled only with the whispery sound of Danny's gentle breathing.

Her words, although soft, filled the room. "I'm the most logical suspect, you know." The emotion had drained from her voice, leaving it with a hollow, metallic echo. "The police know that I had the most to benefit from Bummpt's death." She began to pace the room. "No more visitations. No more listening to his harangues about the 'proper way to raise a McFadden male.' No more arguments about missing child support checks."

"But you didn't do it."

She glanced up in midstep. "How can you be so sure?" Her expression hardened. "Maybe I faked my alibi."

"Even if you did that, I know you didn't kill Bummpt." He raised his hand and ticked off his points. "One—you would have never put your son in jeopardy. Two—you would have never taken a chance of him seeing you do something like that to his father. Three—you wouldn't have hurt Carol because, despite all her faults, she liked Danny and tried to be a good stepmother to him."

Jill said nothing, but she stopped pacing. After a moment, she returned to her son's bed, bracing her hands against the footboard. "You're right. I could never do anything to hurt Danny." After a pause, she drew a deep breath and turned around. "What about your sister?"

It took Matthew by surprise. "What about her?" he asked.

"Aren't you hurting her by not going to visit her?"

He shrugged. "Who says she wants to see me?"

Jill pinned him with a steely gaze. "Who's to say she doesn't want to see you? You won't know until you go upstairs and find out."

"Upstairs? She's here?" So close and he didn't even know it?

"Room 827. I asked."

Matthew stared at the cartoon bear, who looked as if he had not a care in the world. He and Carol had watched Yogi when they were kids together. They'd done lots of things together until...

"Don't stop to think about it." Jill's velvet soft

whisper hid a spine of steel. "Just go upstairs and tell your sister you love her."

"But..."

"No buts. No hesitations. No excuses. Just do it."

TEN MINUTES AND two false starts later, Matthew stood outside of room 827. Another policeman guarded the door, this time, not as big or as apt to jump to conclusions. He checked Matthew's driver's license, paid only mild attention to his press credentials and then allowed him to enter.

Matthew raised his hand to knock on the door then hesitated. If the guard hadn't been standing there, ready to witness Matthew's cowardness, he might have left. But after a moment, he drew the deepest breath he could manage, expelled it in a big whoosh and pushed the door open without knocking.

The room was dark with the exception of a small pool of light in the corner from which a soft clicking noise originated. He panicked for a second or two; machines usually meant some form of artificial support. Heart? Lungs? Both? Was Carol in worse shape than he'd been told?

"Hello, stranger." The clicking stopped and someone shifted into the circle of light.

He felt himself relax. "Whatcha knitting, Mrs. F.?"

Miranda Flynn held out her work for inspection. "Slippers for Carol. She'll need them when she's up and around."

He moved closer to his housekeeper/surrogate mother/caretaker. "When will that be?" His voice clogged uncharacteristically.

"Why don't you ask me, you clod?" Carol's voice was stronger than he expected, sarcastic as ever.

Matthew's gut twisted. "Hey, sis." He moved closer to the head of the bed.

"Turn on the lights. I want to see how old you look."

It was just like Carol, hiding concern beneath a caustic layer. Mrs. Flynn harrumpted as she found a switch to bring up the room lights slowly.

Carol didn't look as good as she sounded. A large bandage covered her neck and the side of her head. It was true; she was a peroxided blonde. It looked terrible on her. Both arms were swathed, including her palms. Matthew had reported on too many crime scenes, seen too many victims not to recognize defensive wounds. Carol had fought for her life and lucky for her, had won.

She eyed him critically. "You don't look too bad. This sabbatical stuff must be agreeing with you."

He started to agree, then stopped. "How did you know about my sabbatical?"

Carol winced as she nodded toward Mrs. Flynn. "We've been talking."

"About me?"

"'Me, me, me,'" she quipped, "Why does everything have to be about you?"

"Now, Carol..." Mrs. Flynn tsk-tsked in a patently motherlike way.

Carol looked elsewhere, suddenly unable to meet his gaze. "We've talked about you. Among other things."

Mrs. Flynn's quiet voice filled the sudden void. "Carolyn has also been talking all about Danny. He sounds like a very nice little boy. She's been quite concerned about him. I told her you might know more."

A warm flush crept up his neck. "He's here, you know."

Carol shifted in bed, growing visibly stiff. "Here? In the hospital?" She glared at Mrs. Flynn. "I thought you said Danny didn't get hurt." She turned her agitated face toward Matthew. "*She* said he was——"

Matthew raised a hand to stop her from working herself into a tirade. "Don't panic. Danny's all right. He wasn't hurt in the attack. He's simply had an asthma attack and evidently, not a particularly serious one at that. Jill's downstairs with him in the Pediatric ward and he's going to stay overnight for observation."

"One problem." Carol's eyes narrowed. "Danny doesn't have asthma."

Matthew pulled the only unoccupied chair closer to the bed and sat down. Talking to his sister was exhausting at best. "Apparently he does. Jill said he'd never had any sort of respiratory problems before. But the doctor told her that he might have always been borderline. If stress could be a contributing factor, then it's no wonder it happened now. The kid has been through a lot. And so has Jill. She's really worried about him."

Carol's panic subsided into a sneer. "So you've met Saint Jill?"

Defensive hackles began to rise across the back of his neck. "Then I take it you don't like her?"

The sneer faded a bit. "She's okay, I guess. And Danny's a real sweet kid. But between the two of them, they really screwed up my marriage. Life would have been a lot easier for me and Dan without having to deal with them, too."

She said her husband's name without flinching,

without emotion, even regret. Was she blocking her true feelings, unwilling as usual to let Matthew into her life or had Bummpt's death freed her at last from an unpleasant marriage?

"I'm...I'm sorry about your husband." Matthew fought the instinct to add, *Of course, I didn't even know you'd married him,* but he knew the remark would likely draw flames from his easily ignited sister.

But the usually energetic, mostly acerbic Carol closed her eyes and drew a shallow breath. "Me, too." After a moment, she opened her eyes. "You didn't even know I was married, did you?"

Rather than unleash a torrent of brotherly concern and admonition, Matthew held himself to a single word.

"No."

Her wan smile didn't quite reach her eyes. "Then I bet it was a real shocker to get my call."

Matthew shrugged. "You could put it that way."

"And an even bigger shock when you came into the house."

Matthew nodded.

Tears began to trickle down one pale cheek. "Not as big as the surprise I had, realizing someone had just killed my husband in our bed." She looked up, blinking. "I don't even remember it, Matt. I don't remember anything at all. Just blood. Lots of blood."

Matthew watched her hands tremble as she fumbled with her blanket. He'd seen several Carols in the past: the militant Carol, the apathetic Carol, the frivolous Carol—but never the scared Carol. Everything he'd ever felt for her as a child came rushing back to the surface. He wanted to comfort her, protect her and become her brother again, a role he thought he'd been forced by her to forsake years ago.

But he also knew Carol well. If he unleashed a deluge of emotion, she'd pull away as usual. After all these years, she was probably even less accustomed to dealing with brotherly love and concern, likely mistaking it for pity just as she had in the past. So he did the next best thing; he changed the subject, somewhat.

He leaned closer to her, placing his forearms on the bed railing. "You want to know what a real shock is?" He rested his chin on his arms and sighed. "I thought Danny was your son."

Carol stared at him, unaware of the fresh cascade of tears coursing down her cheeks. An odd light lit her face. "Danny? Mine? My son?"

He nodded. "Six years is a long time. Who knows what could have happened during then? It was entirely possible that you'd made me an uncle. That night...for a short while, I had a nephew and you know what?" He didn't wait for her response. "It was scary as hell. I mean...here was this little guy, alone at the moment, frightened, confused. But you should have seen the look of relief that crossed his face when I told him I thought I was his Uncle Matt." He couldn't help but remember the feeling of Danny's death grip around his neck.

"Uncle Matt." Carol repeated the words as if she were testing them, weighing them. She looked up in amazement. "You really thought he was mine?"

Matthew nodded. "I did. And what really surprised me was how ready I was to accept him and take responsibility for him. I haven't thought much about having kids, but Danny..." His voice trailed off.

"I know what you mean." Carol drew a deep

breath. "When he'd come for visitation, Dan would always find some reason to leave him with me. Hell, I spent more time with the kid than Bummpt did. Anyways, when it'd be just Danny and me, sometimes I'd pretend he was my kid. And you know what?" A look of sentimental sweetness filled her face, a look that Matthew thought he'd never see again.

"What?" he croaked.

"I liked it. I liked it a whole lot. But I guess that's another busted dream, right?"

Matthew couldn't respond. There were no words in him at the moment.

"I'm tired of dreams becoming nightmares, Matt."

He almost reached over to pat her hand, but something stopped him. Not her bandages, but the desire not to push the new reconnection between them.

Her lips trembled and tears filled her eyes. "Mattie?"

It was the second time she'd used that nickname, something she'd called him when he was little. The first time was during the phone call when she was hurt, confused and scared. Why now?

"Yeah, Carol?"

"Something bad happened."

He glanced at Mrs. Flynn, wondering if they should call a doctor of something. Carol was starting to sound…odd. Mrs. Flynn merely shook her head, then pointed back to Carol.

He turned back to his sister. "What's wrong, honey?"

She looked up, her eyes not quite focusing on him. "Bummpt's dead and I lost my baby."

The news hit him like a sledgehammer in the gut. "Baby?" he whispered hoarsely.

She nodded, suddenly dry-eyed. "I was three months pregnant and I miscarried yesterday."

"Oh, Carol…" It all sounded so weak, so empty, but he'd never meant anything as much as he did at the moment. "I'm so sorry."

Her bottom lip quivered and she looked straight at him for the first time in six years.

"Me, too."

Chapter Ten

Jill was only half-asleep when Matthew walked into the hospital room. But she awoke completely after a brief glance at his dark expression. Something had gone wrong, terribly wrong.

"What?" she demanded, rising from the chair. "Your sister's not..." She covered her mouth, unable to say the word *dead*. There had been too much death around them already.

He shook his head. "No, she's going to be okay." His hooded glare softened a bit as he stared at her son. "Danny looks better."

"He's—" Normally, she would have said "dead asleep," but the word caught in her throat. "—asleep. They gave him a mild sedative and said he'd be out until morning."

"What about you?" He nodded toward her make-shift bed. "You can't be comfortable in a chair."

She tried to twist the latest kink out of her neck. "It's not the Ritz Carlton, but I like the proximity to my son."

"Oh." His somber expression remained intact, signifying perhaps that he'd hoped for a different answer. The garish decorations seemed to capture his attention for a moment, then she realized that his gaze was unfocused.

"There's something...more," she prompted, stating the obvious, rather than inquiring about it.

He shrugged. "I was just going to ask you if you were up to taking a little walk."

She hesitated before answering. To take a walk meant being away from Danny.

At her moment of indecision, he added, "Not far, just down the corridor. I know you don't want to leave Danny alone for long."

It was a matter of balancing the needs of two people, Jill decided. Matthew evidently needed to talk, but then there was Danny.

Sweet Danny.

She stared at her son, measuring his even breath, taking comfort with his look of contentment in sleep as he curled around his beloved Mr. Popster. The doctor had assured her that Danny wouldn't be waking any time soon. Maybe a walk might be good for her. It might provide her a chance to work out some of the knots in her back.

And Matthew?

She allowed herself the luxury of looking at him, not just a quick glimpse or a darting glance, but a long, searching gaze that almost bordered on an impolite stare. What she saw was a man who desperately needed to get something off his chest. He fidgeted, shifted his weight from one foot to the other. Something indeed was bothering him.

Why did she care? Why did she feel a need to help him deal with his own tragedies when hers were just as overwhelming? When she looked into his deep brown eyes, she marveled at the man within, someone willing to care, someone kind, supportive…

Loving…

She slipped her hand in his. "Let's go."

After informing the guard that she wasn't going far and receiving his response in the form of a quick nod, she and Matthew walked in silence to the end of the hallway, his hand remained wrapped almost protectively around hers. As they reached the window at the end of the hall, he stopped suddenly. Although he gazed out the window, she knew his mind, his thoughts were somewhere else.

After a few moments, his grip grew slack and he spoke in a raspy voice. "I thought maybe she'd changed. I thought that maybe in six years, she'd grown up some. But Carol hasn't changed much. She's still cocksure hers is the only way. Still defensive, edgy…" His voice trailed off for a moment. "She still likes to shock people."

"Everybody?" Jill watched the muscles in his jaw clench. "Or maybe just you?"

"Everybody. *Especially* me." His lips set in a thin line and he stared harder out the window at nothing in particular. Then, in an abrupt move, he released Jill's hand, breaking contact with her as if a physical separation would help him achieve the emotional isolation he so desperately needed.

As he braced his palms against the windowsill, Jill watched a myriad of emotions cross his face, transforming his expression of great disappointment to one of great anger in the course of only a few seconds. At the height of his emotion, he closed his eyes and knotted one hand into a fist.

Jill stared at his fist and her blood suddenly ran cold.

Memories flashed through her mind, forbidden images that she'd thought she'd managed to push into a forgotten corner of her mind.

It would be a familiar sequence of events; a man's disappointment always turned to anger. Vague obscenities hurled at the world in general would eventually congeal into specific complaints, needing a handy target. As the anger grew in size and gained a sense of direction, it would escalate into full-fledged, no-holds-barred rage.

Aimed directly at her.

If you can't be with the one you hate, hate the one you're with, had been Bummpt's motto. And he hated lots of people.

And when his rage erupted, the only way to abate it was to act out his frustrations on the nearest person: her.

Anger equated pain. It had been a simple and infallible formula, a constant in her universe.

She watched Matthew's fist intently, waiting for the inescapable collision when mounting fury met a pane of glass. Whoever said "full of sound and fury, signifying nothing" had no idea what it was like to be in the direct path of escalating wrath.

But to her utter surprise, he unclenched his fist and his harsh expression shattered rather than the glass.

Something else shattered in her as well.

No pain. No hurled accusations that might not make sense, but hurt nonetheless. No bruises, no words of degradation, no "punctuation marks" as Bummpt had called the marks he'd left.

All of the sudden, Jill was no longer afraid. Two facts had become crystal clear to her: she'd never have to fear Bummpt again, and she'd never have a reason to fear Matthew. The revelation made her almost giddy with relief, but she sobered quickly, realizing that although Matthew's wrath had passed, his pain remained.

He released a deep sigh as he stared out the window. "Carol was pregnant," he said in a flat voice.

It took several seconds for Jill to digest the news. *Was pregnant*... "You mean she lost...?"

He nodded. "Miscarried because of the attack."

"Oh, Matthew..." She reached out and touched his arm, feeling tensed muscles beneath that she tried not to fear. "That's terrible. How is she doing?"

He shrugged and turned away, leaning so that his forehead rested against the pane of glass. "With Carol, it's hard to tell. I don't know if it was a planned pregnancy or an accident. All I know is, it's over. I don't know if she's sad, or relieved or angry or what. Just like always, she refused to let me in, to share these things with me."

Jill shifted behind him, wrapping her arms around his waist and resting her face on his back in a backward sort of hug. They stood there for a while without speaking, letting the comfort of close contact express all the things that could not be said aloud.

A droplet fell on her hands and she realized he was crying, quietly, privately. She joined him.

They remained there, silently, their burdens shared and therefore halved. After several minutes passed, Matt turned around in her embrace, wrapping his own arms around her. He rested his chin on her shoulder.

He spoke with a wistful bitterness. "I could have been an Uncle Matt...for real. But someone took that away from us." His hug tightened into something almost painful. Suddenly cognizant of this, he pulled back so that they stood toe-to-toe, eye to eye.

He brushed her hair back with a gentle gesture. "Up to now, I was simply helping Danny, helping you because that's what I do—I help people because someone once helped me. But now, this has become my problem, too. It's gotten...personal."

Jill nodded.

"I'm going to find the person who did this, and make him pay."

Retribution? She felt her protective hackles rise. "That doesn't mean you're going to try to play vigilante, is it?"

A thin furrow appeared between his brows. "Vigilante? Me?" he croaked. The harsh lines in his face faded as his dark expression lightened. "No way. I'm not stupid." He clenched his hand into a fist and stared at it intently. "This won't get me very far." Then he uncurled his forefinger from his fist and used it to tap his temple. "I'll be a lot more successful if I use my brain instead. I'm an investigative reporter. I know how to sit back and rearrange the pieces of the puzzle to come up with a solution. My motto is 'Brains over brawn, whenever possible.'"

Jill relaxed her grip on his waist and nodded. "I agree entirely."

"In fact—" he broke her embrace gently and twined his fingers in hers "—I was working on a couple of theories when I got the call about Danny."

"What sort of theories?"

"Just some ideas I'd like to run past you, if you don't mind."

A nurse stepped out of a nearby room and gave both Jill and Matthew a censuring glare and they fell appropriately quiet. As the woman left, Matthew spoke in a lowered voice. "But evidently, this isn't the place. Could you stand being away from Danny long enough to go downstairs and get a cup of coffee?"

Jill paused for a moment, reminding herself of the doctor's proclamation that her son would be out for hours.

As if reading her concern, Matthew nodded. "I know, I know. Leaving Danny..." He shook his head, then brightened quickly. "What about my house-keeper, Mrs. Flynn? She's upstairs visiting with Carol. What if I ask her to come down here for a while and stay with Danny while we talk? Even if he woke up, he'd feel comfortable around Mrs. F. Kids always fall instantly in love with her—she has this real grand-mother-type thing going for her."

A few minutes later, Jill found herself in a com-forting, grandmotherly embrace—one that smelled vaguely of gingerbread, eau de violets and the slightest hint of mothballs. Matthew was right; Danny would instantly love this woman with her sensible shoes, her uneven stockings and her lace handkerchief pinned to her dress with a Star Trek communicator pin.

"Now don't you worry about a thing," she assured in a quiet voice. "I'll watch over Danny and every-thing will be fine." She beamed at the guard who stood stiffly at the door. "With this strapping young man to protect us, nothing will go wrong. Right, hand-some?" She patted his gun arm.

The policeman's face reddened slightly as he cracked a small smile. "Yes'm."

She turned to Jill. "I'll page you in the cafeteria if he wakes up, okeydokey?"

"Thanks, Mrs. F." Matthew leaned over and pecked her on the cheek.

Jill and Matthew rode down in the elevator in an agreeable silence, both evidently willing to wait until they had coffee and a quiet table before they started any important discussions. After they settled themselves, Jill took a fortifying sip of her coffee and gave her chocolate-dipped doughnut a dubious stare. "I don't know why I bought this."

Matthew leaned down and gave it a careful once-over. "I suspect you bought it because that old adage is really true."

"What old adage?"

He conjured up a passable grin. "You know... 'Misery loves chocolate.'"

She stared at him. He was making a joke. After all of this, all the loss, the pain, the unanswered questions...he could still make a joke. She returned what she wished could be something more than a pale imitation of his smile, but despite the fact that she appreciated his attempt at humor, her heart simply wasn't into it. Her heart was upstairs with her son.

He reached toward her, perhaps to pat her hand, or maybe to hold it. But he must have had second thoughts about the intimacy of the gesture and quickly diverted his motion and grabbed his coffee, instead. He concerned himself with warming his face over the steaming brew. "Sorry. Self-defense mechanism. When all else fails, make a joke."

She nodded, accepting his apology. "I understand. So what did you find out at the paper?"

He made a face and put his cup down without tasting its content. "I started going through our files and pulling out information on any knife-related death in the last six months.''

Jill glanced down at the white plastic knife, half hidden by her doughnut. Any hunger she might have possessed was now completely gone. ''A knife...''

Matthew reached over, plucked the offending utensil from the tray and tossed it over to a cluttered table. ''It's become the most viable link between several murders, which leads me to think the deaths might have all been caused by the same person.''

Jill cocked her head in thought. ''But knives aren't like guns. With guns, they can do all sorts of ballistic tests and measure the actual markings on the bullets. You can't do that with a knife, can you?''

''Actually, they can. The forensic guys can perform a test that charts and identifies the blade based on the cuts and markings it left behind. In this particular case, the blade was serrated which means it left a very obvious pattern in whatever material it cut.'' He pushed on, not willing to pause and let her contemplate that flesh was considered a material in this instance. ''Plus, it had a couple of unique nicks and scraps in the blade which will make it even easier to identify and track. Find the person with the knife and you've found the killer.''

She picked at a crumb that had fallen off her doughtnut. ''So if all these people were killed by one man, one knife, then there must be some sort of connection between the victims.''

He nodded. ''It could be something as simple as the killer had a grudge against them all. Or something as innocuous as they shopped at the same stores, belonged to the same clubs. What I have to do is find the connection, find the pattern.''

Finding a pattern sounded harmless enough, but what were the chances Matthew would only be looking at dry facts and figures rather than a man with a knife in his hand? "I don't think you ought to get this involved. It's a job for the police, not for you."

"So far, the police haven't made the connection of the knife with all the deaths. It looks like I may be a step ahead of them."

"Then tell them," she urged, her heart starting to beat more furiously. "Tell them everything." *I don't want any more reasons to worry. Or mourn...*

He shook his head. "Don't worry about that, I'll tell them everything I know about all of the murders."

"All the murders," she repeated. "How many... deaths are we talking about?

He stared at his untouched coffee. "So far, I've found three other men whose deaths involved a knife, directly or indirectly. It'll take a forensics guy to figure out if it's definitely the same knife, but I'm willing to work from the assumption that it's one knife and one knife means one killer. The question becomes—why these four men? What did Bummpt and these guys have in common?"

Jill knitted her brow in concentration. "Who are they? Maybe he knew them. Or worked with them."

A familiar voice intruded on their conversation. "Or had something else in common with them."

They both jumped.

"Or someone."

Sid Morrison shot them a tight smile that didn't quite reach his eyes. "Sorry, didn't mean to scare you." He glanced down at Matthew, who remained seated. "Your office told me you were here." The policeman turned to Jill and she fought the urge to jump to her feet. "I was just up in your son's room. I know you'll be glad to learn he's still asleep." Sid paused and then his smile grew more genuine and perhaps, just a bit sad. "I'm sorry the little fellow's ailing."

"The little fellow's ailing?"

Matthew stared at the lieutenant. Why the homespun-sheriff routine? Matthew's protective instincts went on well-honed alert. When Sid Morrison played Sheriff Andy Taylor, it meant heads were about to roll.

Sid pulled out a chair and sat down by Jill. "Mrs. McFadden, I'm afraid we—"

"Kincaid," she corrected automatically.

He was slightly taken aback, but managed to nod affably. "Of course, Ms. Kincaid." He stressed the word *Ms.* as if it were an amusing concept recently coined by uppity women. All Sid needed now was a corncob pipe to finish the unflattering stereotype. But Matthew knew it was nothing more than Sid's typical ruse to disarm the people he interrogated, to throw them off their timing so that they were apt to either tell the truth or make their lies easier to spot.

But why was he doing it to Jill? Did he suddenly consider her a suspect?

The unfortunate answer came only a moment later.

"Would you mind stepping over to the door and answering a few questions from my colleague, Mr. McNeil?" He pointed to Cotton McNeil who stood near the food line, eyeing a row of pastries and not watching for his lieutenant's signal. Sid stiffened a bit. "McNeil!"

Cotton turned sharply, a bit of color flaring in his usually pale face. He managed to get to the table quickly, but couldn't avoid looking as if he were a dog following his master's orders.

Jill rose slowly, giving Matthew a quick, covered look that said, "I don't like this," but also hiding a flare of amusement.

Good, Matthew thought. She recognized Sid's mind games for what they were— disarming techniques. Matthew nodded in acknowledgment, but his good spirits faded when Sid plopped down in Jill's vacant chair.

Matthew suddenly knew that the person who needed to be disarmed and misdirected was himself. And damn it, he hadn't seen it coming.

Sid raised his hand and started counting on his fingers.

One: "Daniel 'Bummpt' McFadden."

Obviously.

Two: "Vernon McCreedy."

Someone had been doing his homework.

Three: "Billy McCreedy."

Matthew decided it was time to speak. "The stock car brothers. So?"

Four: "Nelson Chandler."

Then to Matthew's surprise, Sid lifted this thumb as number five. "Phoebe Robinson."

Matthew scrambled to put a face to the name. "Phoebe…"

"Robinson," Sid supplied. "Better known as The Evil Queen. You know…in that cartoon?"

Matthew thought back to last summer's big box office hit, a feature-length animated movie. It was typical kiddie fairy-tale fare with a handsome prince, a politically correct princess who helped slay the fiery dragon and of course, the obligatory Evil Queen, all voices by various Hollywood stars on their way up or down the celebrity success ladder. Phoebe Robinson was firmly anchored around a middle rung of that ladder, a once-upon-a-time leading lady of stage and screen who was keeping her post-ingenue career very much alive and kicking by taking character roles. But unfortunately, Phoebe Robinson was no longer alive and kicking.

"Phoebe Robinson wasn't murdered," Matthew corrected. "She died of natural causes."

"A heart attack. But the question isn't what caused that heart attack, but who? And why?" He held up five fingers. "Why all of them? Who wanted all of them dead?"

Matthew watched the lieutenant intently. "Then you think this is the work of one man."

"Man?" A small smile creased Sid's face. "Why, Matthew, I didn't know you were a chauvinist. The killer could quite possibly be a woman." He glanced in Jill's direction.

"C'mon, Sid. Surely you don't think—"

He waved his hand to stop Matthew in midsentence. "It doesn't matter what I think. What matters are the facts. And the facts are we have five, maybe six victims."

"Six?" Matthew straightened in his chair. "Who's the sixth one?"

Sid shook his head. "Nope, I'm keeping that one close to vest, right now. But suffice it to say, the M.E. is looking into it."

"Then it's a recent death?"

Sid shook his head again. "Sorry. I know all your reporter tricks. And speaking of newspapers, something has come up in this investigation which…'' Sid's voice trailed off.

Matthew waited for him to finish. ''Well?''

''There's another connection between all these cases.'' Sid studied the doughnut Jill had left behind. ''Besides the knife, that is.''

Matthew expelled his breath. ''Then you know about the knife.'' A moment later, he realized his fatigue had allowed him to fall for the oldest trick in the book.

Sid nodded, his lips set in a slightly triumphal smirk. ''When were you going to tell us? Tomorrow? The next day? Next week?''

Matthew sighed. ''That's what we were discussing before we were so rudely interrupted. So what's come up with your investigation?''

Sid stared blankly at the table, then lifted his gaze. ''Where were you on September 6 of this year?''

The question caught Matthew by surprise. ''September 6? I…I don't know. I'd need my calendar and—'' He paused, belatedly realizing the implications. ''Aw, Sid…you don't think. C'mon, that's ridiculous.''

There wasn't a single shred of amusement in the policeman's face as he stood. ''Why don't we talk about this at the station?'' He all but clamped a restraining hand on Matthew's biceps.

''The station? But…'' Matthew rose as well and pivoted, spotting Jill, who stood beside Cotton, her arms wrapped protectively around herself. She looked scared about something. Scared about someone. About him? His stomach twisted. ''Jill, I—''

Sid stood between them. ''Don't worry about the lady, Matt, my boy. Cotton will see her safely back to her son's room.''

Matthew felt every muscle in his body tense. "Sid, you don't honestly think—"

Sid cut him off with a wave of his hand. "Like I told you before, it doesn't matter what *I* think. You prove you weren't around when Ms. Robinson was killed and that'll be a start."

Matthew shook his head, hoping to reorder thoughts that shock had scrambled. "This is ridiculous, you know. It's a matter of motive and opportunity. I have no motive to kill someone like her. Or any of those people."

Sid smiled, evidently ready to play his trump card. "Then why are you the only connection between all these people?"

"Me?"

Sid reached in coat pocket and pulled out some papers. He flattened them on the table, revealing them to be photocopy of a newspaper column.

"Notice anything about this?"

Matthew picked up the paper and stared at it, recognizing the title. It was one of his best pieces, an award-winning article that came out five years ago, one which addressed the changing atmosphere of crime from a child's perspective.

"The Death of Things that Go Bump in the Night."

Sid slid the paper out of Matthew's grasp. "You and me. We need to go down to the station."

Chapter Eleven

Matthew and Sid sat across from each other, almost at a stalemate. The papers in question, slightly curled from being clenched in Sid's sweaty hand, sat exactly halfway between them on the scarred table, partially obscuring a set of crudely carved initials. Sid slid the papers over so that they lined up neatly, perpendicular with the lines of the tabletop. He'd always had a proclivity to exact order and an eye for detail. Why he and the ever rumpled Cotton, the Oscar Madison of detectives, worked well together was one of the great unsolved mysteries of the universe.

The Odd Couple Meets Police Squad.

"When did you write this?" Sid tapped the paper with an impatient forefinger.

Matthew pointed to the date at the top of the page which was upside down to him. "It's printed right here."

"The date," Sid prompted. He pointed to the tape recorder which spun silently beside them.

Matthew reigned in a sigh before it escaped. The recorder was only more of Sid's disarming techniques. "March 25, 1993."

"Read this section."

Matthew turned the paper around, watching as Sid reacted with distaste to the disruption of order. Matthew began to read to himself.

Sid cleared his throat and made a don't-screw-with-me face. "Aloud, if you don't mind."

Matthew allowed himself the unrestrained sigh he held moments ago, cleared his throat and began to read aloud.

"'Once upon a time, all we had to fear as children was fear itself. The monsters of yesteryear sprang from the unrestrained imagination of children, but in today's world, the things that—'" Matthew tried to keep the rising emotion from his voice "'—go bump in the night just may kill you if you don't kill them first.'" The words, ones he had once thought were clever, now seemed damned ominous.

He lowered the paper. "Surely you don't think—"

Sid made a brushing gesture with his hand, encouraging him to continue. "It's a beginning. Let's just called it, 'One.' Skip down to the next paragraph."

Matthew tried not to crumple the paper, but his fingers wanted to tighten around something. "Sid, the wording is only a coincidence. It's nothing more than an article about violent crimes perpetrated on children."

Sid wore no telltale expression, other than mild revelation. "Next paragraph."

Matthew read, "'Whereas in earlier idyllic times, children had only to fear a needle in a doctor's office, needles are finding their way into schoolyards across the nation with increasing numbers. And between lethal designer drugs and incurable diseases such as AIDS, a simple prick from a needle can mean certain death in today's world.'"

Sid crossed his arms. "Nelson Chandler owned a hospital supply company and one of their big stock items is needles." Something akin to a chilled smile crossed his face. "That's two…coincidences."

Matthew felt his hackles rise along with a healthy case of what might be considered deadly curiosity. If this was the work of someone else, he'd be equally as intrigued, as skeptical.

As condemning.

He scanned the article, reading his own words in a new, deadly light.

I spoke recently with a ten-year old girl—

"Aloud," Sid prompted again.

"'I spoke recently with a ten-year old girl from the inner city who had miraculously survived four drive-by shootings in the last six months. She described a street gun battle with the same sense of inevitability as a lightning storm—full of thunderous explosions and deadly bolts of lightning, striking without warning and with lethal consequences.'"

Sid held up four fingers. "That makes three and four. Thunder and Lightning—the McCreedy Boys. You know what four coincidences make, don't you?" He folded his fingers down. "A pattern."

Matthew crumpled the paper in a tight fist. "Sid…this is crazy. You don't think—"

"That you telegraphed your intentions to murder a slew of people in a newspaper article?" Sid leaned forward in his chair. "Jeez, Childs, that sort of stuff only happens in the movies. I believe you." He shifted back. "However, the district attorney would feel a lot better if you would could tell us where you were on these dates." Sid reached into his jacket yet again, this time pulling out a small piece of paper with a short list of numbers.

Matthew looked into Sid's expressionless face, then stared down at the paper. The numbers swam before his eyes. "I'll need a calendar."

A wall calendar slapped lightly to the desk.

"No, not just any calendar. My calendar. At home in my office."

Sid grimaced. "I figured you say that." He stood up, jingling keys in pants pocket. "C'mon...let's go."

"No warrant?"

Sid raised an eyebrow. "Do I need one?"

SID GLANCED AROUND at the pictures that filled the office walls. Matthew had felt self-conscious about his unusual decorations before, but for the first time, he wondered what sort of man lived in an office three-quarters covered with pictures of a crime scene.

Sid stared at a blood-splattered close-up. "I think you need a new decorator." He stepped closer to another photo and gave it unusually close inspection. "That your dad?"

Matthew pretended to study the computer. He knew the photo all too well—the only "normal" picture in the room. It was a candid snapshot of his father, taken about two weeks before his murder.

Matthew covered his discomfort with a noncommittal "Uh-huh."

"Shame what happened to him. You were young, weren't you?"

He bit back a less-tempered response. "Too young."

Sid uttered a rumble of agreement, then turned back to the computer which was flickering to life. "Well?"

"The program's loading." A few moments later, Matthew sighed. "There." A calendar page sprang into existence on the screen. Drawing a sharp breath, he consulted Sid's list of dates in question. There was no need to discuss the day Bummpt was murdered, he'd already offered that alibi. So he skipped down to the next date: January 22, 1998.

He didn't need any prompting to know whose deaths occurred on this date. He'd been scheduled to start his sabbatical the following week, but his editor had coerced him to hang around to handle some of the initial stories about the untimely dual deaths of the stock car driving McCreedys.

It hadn't been all that long ago. He almost didn't need a calendar to remember that he'd been home fighting what he thought had been a wicked hangover from a Wednesday hump-day party that had turned out to be the flu.

"I was home sick." As he spoke, he realized the explanation sounded less like the truth and more like a very poorly executed alibi.

Lame, Childs, very lame.

Judging by the look on Sid's face, the detective agreed wholeheartedly. The lieutenant almost smirked. "I'll need a note from your doctor."

"Would my housekeeper do?" Matthew countered. "She found me in the bathroom where I was trying not to pass out. I'm sure she remembers the whole thing more vividly than I do. She cleaned up after me."

"Did she stay with you all night?" To Sid's credit, there wasn't a single bit of lasciviousness in his question. Chances were he'd met Mrs. Flynn in Danny's hospital room.

Matthew stretched sore muscles. "Honestly? I have no idea." As soon as the words hit the air, he realized his strategic error; it paid to be exact when trying to alibi one's self, especially in the face of what would probably equate to multiple capital murder charges.

"Uh…I mean…" His mind went blank.

Funny how he could think clearly and rationally when, as a reporter, he was the one asking the questions. But now that he was the one required to supply the answers, things grew awfully complicated. He made one last effort.

"You have to understand—I was sick. Out of it pretty much the whole day."

Sid crossed his arms. "I'll pretend I didn't hear that half-assed excuse. And you can be sure I'll talk to your housekeeper later. But I want to go on to the second date." He consulted the list of dates. "September 6, 1997."

Matthew pulled up the date on his calendar. It was a Saturday, which meant a day off from the office and most likely, a day spent hunched over the home computer, working on his book. At that point in time, he was still working full-time, and became an aspiring novelist only on his days off.

Pulling up his work log, he realized with a stab of surprise, he'd logged no time that day, writing. And with a grimace, he relayed the information to Sid, adding a pale caveat of, "I must have been out, running errands."

Sid remained the great stoneface. "No alibi, huh?"

A trickle of electricity crept up Matthew's spine. Where had he been? What had he—

Errands!

A minute later, he'd pulled up the financial program

he used to keep track of his business expenses. There he found several entries: $12.85 to a local printer, $189.38 to an office supply warehouse and $6.40 at the post office. None of these expenses raised a mental flag until he got to the last entry: dinner for two at La Cartier.

Now he remembered.

That day, he'd only meant to get a case of paper, but the woman he met at the office supply store, a siren by the name of Jaycie, had been charming.

Too charming.

Matthew glanced ruefully at the box tossed in the corner of the room. Almost nine months later and he *still* hadn't installed the modem he'd bought from her. But he certainly remembered in crystal clear detail the dinner they'd shared that night. By the time they reached their crème brûlée, he was certain something wonderful was happening between them. And they did have a glorious and rather adventurous two months together until her old boyfriend came back to town.

Matthew suddenly learned that absence had indeed made the heart grow fonder and he had been, in her own words, "a pleasant way station on her road to fulfillment." Just call him Pitstop Pete on the road of love.

He tried to conjure up the memory of her face, but an image of Jill insisted on dominating his thoughts, banishing all competition.

Competition?

Well, maybe. At least he hoped so.

It wasn't charm that attracted him to Jill. He'd met his share of charming but vapid women. It wasn't her good looks, even though she ranked right up there on the list of Pretty Women I've Met. And it wasn't necessarily a damsel in distress situation. He'd never been much good at rescuing the distressed damsel and he suspected that Jill wouldn't relish being thought of in that manner.

He liked her because...

He really liked her a great deal because...

"Well?" Sid's voice intruded on his thoughts. "I take it that the person who can verify where you were that night was a woman?"

Matthew felt his face redden. "Yeah."

A smirk crossed the policeman's face. "Were you good enough in bed for her to still remember you, now?"

Matthew made a rather pointed gesture of clearing the monitor screen. "A gentleman never tells."

Sid leaned forward slightly in the chair. "He does if he doesn't want to spend the night in central lockup."

After only a split second of hesitation, Matthew pulled up his address database, found Jaycie's address and phone number, printing it off for Sid. "She's married now, so try not to bring her husband into this."

Sid took the paper and folded it neatly. "Was she married during the time?"

Matthew straightened in his chair. "No."

"Good. I'll try to talk only to her. Next?"

The other alibis were much easier to root out and luckily, none were quite as personal as the first one. No old girlfriends. No moments of being indisposed due to health, desire or anything else of an emotional nature.

What really surprised Matthew was how well he could dredge up his life in terms of computer files. It was if his entire life revolved around the computer. Evidently, Sid made the connection as well.

The policeman scanned the dozen or so pages that Matthew had printed out for him which detailed the various places he'd been when the murders had occurred.

"Neat. Complete. I wish I could get all my cases delivered to me in twelve-point Courier laser print." He glanced up at Matthew and his face emptied of all sarcasm. "You really ought to get a life."

Matthew leaned back in his chair and stretched tensed muscles. "I know."

Sid folded the rest of the papers and stuffed them in his jacket pocket. "Well, you ought to at least be pleased to know that I don't really think you're a serial killer."

Matthew pointed to Sid's chest, the current location of some of the more critical facts and figures that hopefully cleared his good name. "Then why put me though all this? Why all the factoids? The names, the dates..."

Sid shot him a rueful smile. "The D.A. doesn't want to rely purely on my instincts about a case. I have been known to make mistakes, before." After a moment, he added, "Only on rare occasions, that is. But I figure if you were the real sicko who's doing this, you'd have worked in the other deaths in your column. There's nothing about an Evil Queen or the other death."

"Other death." Matthew's reporter instincts swam to the surface. "When are you going to tell me about the sixth victim?"

"No time soon. I know not to spill everything to a reporter."

"But I'm on leave of absence."

"Once a newsman, always a newsman. Your editor said those very words to me when we called him, looking for you." Sid plowed his hand through his thinning hair. "Listen, we have to keep some details about the killings under wraps—to weed out the Confession Queens."

Matthew knew of at least two nutcases in town who arrived Johnny-on-the-spot to confess to the latest act of crime, be it murder, rape or armed robbery. Some of them had gotten rather good at researching the cases and working up a suitable confession of guilt. Trouble was, you never knew when or if one of them might fall completely out of their tree and get inspired to cause the crime as well as own up to it.

Well, Matthew Childs was good at researching cases, too. "You do know it's not going to take much for me to get a name. I know the MO…and that's a big start."

Sid shook his head. "You don't know nearly as much as you think you do. Sure, you know about the knife, but remember, our boy has already found inspiration outside of your article. Even if you start checking for unsolved murders involving a knife, you don't have the city. Or the state. And considering the number of violent deaths that occur daily in the United States…"

Matthew raised his hand in mock surrender. "Okay, okay. I understand. You want to keep an ace up your sleeve. No problem. But at the risk of talking myself back into contention as a potential suspect, are you sure the other deaths are related? The Evil Queen and this new one?"

"It's the same knife in both. I don't know how we

missed the connection, especially with the Robinson case.''

Matthew thought back on the publicity that had swirled around the woman's untimely death. No one had even whispered the word *murder* in connection with it. "I thought the official report was that she died of a heart attack.''

"She did. It happened while she was in the hospital, supposedly preparing to get plastic surgery. But she was actually there for the doctors to run some tests on her heart. Evidently, she'd suffered from some sort of attack a week earlier and they were trying to determine how much damage had been done to her heart and how much blockage still existed. Such a beautiful woman...a real classy dame by all accounts. You know that she donated her paycheck from that last kiddie movie to some children's charity?''

Sid drew a deep breath, the brief flash of admiration fading from his eyes. "What a waste." He shook his head, then picked up where he'd left off. "So when she died, no one suspected that the cause was anything other than an unfortunate, fatal heart attack. Then, a postmortem revealed that not only had she died of a heart attack, but someone had attempted to suffocate her, probably triggering the heart attack to begin with.'' He shook his head. "By the time they called us, the room had been cleaned since no one had considered it to be a crime scene. But I did find something interesting left behind in the room.''

Matthew's interest was piqued. "What?''

"The nurse who found her body said that the patient couldn't have used the nurses' call button because it had slipped out of her reach. One of the plastic ties that held it in place was gone, allowing the button to fall out of Ms. Robinson's reach. Later, I found a piece of the plastic strap and the forensic guys say it's definitely been cut with—"

"A knife with an oddly serrated blade," Matthew supplied.

"Exactly. There's not enough of the cut to make a sure identification with the other articles, but they don't all have to be strikes. I'll take a spare or two, every now and then. What worries me the most is the fact that our man is starting to cross some unusual barriers, to widen his selection of victims."

"Widen?" Matthew ran through a mental list of victims. Bummpt, the two McCreedy brothers, Mr. Chandler, Ms. Robinson... Ms....

"A female victim," he said slowly.

Sid nodded. "And it gets worse from there."

Matthew stared at the man. "Worse? In what way?"

"I can't tell you," Sid muttered as he shifted toward the door. He stopped there and drummed his fingers against the door frame. "Aw, damn...it doesn't go any further than this room. No forty-point headlines. No anonymous calls to the city desk about this clown, okay?"

Matthew pulled to his feet. "Scout's honor. What, Sid?"

The lieutenant closed his eyes and shook his head. "Not only did he cross a gender barrier, but now he's crossed a racial one as well."

He released a world-weary sigh.

"The sixth victim is black."

Chapter Twelve

The psychologist spoke in a quiet but eloquent voice, one much too mellifluous for the subject matter.

"The average serial killer is a white male, between the ages of twenty-five and thirty-five. His intellectual ability ranges anywhere from below average to above average. He seldom crosses racial boundaries when selecting victims, however his victims' ages may vary greatly. He harbors no particular hatred for his victims nor did they ever do anything to hurt him. It is highly likely he may not know them at all. He comes from no particular social class or strata nor do his victims."

Jill listened numbly to the doctor. "That makes it sound as if it could be any man." She glanced at the white-haired detective who stood in the doorway, his arms crossed. A shiver coursed up her spine and spread across her shoulders.

"These are just broad characteristics. Profiling is the art of identifying common characteristics and behaviors of serial killers and using the similarities as a technique to help identify other serial—"

"Hold it." Jill narrowed her gaze. "Why are you telling me this?"

The psychologist turned to Cotton McNeil, who responded by flushing an unattractive bright red.

Jill stared at the policeman, fear solidifying into something unappetizing in her stomach. "Why are you making him tell me all this?"

Cotton twitched, then after a few moments, made a silent, go-ahead motion to the blue-coated doctor. The man cleared his throat. "As I was saying…as a child, he may have suffered some sort of devastating trauma."

The words sunk in.

"W-what kind of trauma?"

"Most frequently, one of a sexual nature. A situation of abuse."

"Or…" Cotton prompted in a leading tone.

The doctor took his cue. "Or, in some instances, an exposure to traumatic violence."

Jill's heart caught in her throat. "You think my son might become a serial—"

The doctor's eyes widened. "No, no!" He shook his head violently. "I mean nothing of the sort. I'm not talking about your son, Ms. Kincaid."

"Then why in the world are you telling me this?" She stared at the doctor who said nothing and suddenly diverted his attention to the clipboard. Then she glared at the detective who silently turned a deeper shade of red.

The doctor cleared his throat. "Um…it's not unusual to d-discover that the killer has a fascination with law enforcement officials. He may attempt to hang around with them, befriend them, study them—" he paused for a moment, making uncomfortable eye contact with her "—even…write about them."

Write?

It hit her.

"Matthew?" Her stomach performed several flip-flops. "You think he's…" She couldn't finish the sentence. She couldn't even finish the thought. The mere effort of breathing became impossible as bands of panic tightened around her chest. As she slipped under the churning surface of panic, dread filled her lungs with the same efficiency as water in a drowning pool. She fought for air and for self-control.

Not Matthew.

Why not? Her inner voice prodded. *He fits their profile.*

But I know him. I like him. And Danny likes him. The word *like* had never sounded so inadequate before.

Like? Love? So what? Once upon a long time ago, you loved Bummpt. He only made you wish you were dead. Matthew could actually do it.

As if reading her thoughts, the doctor gestured with open palms. "Let's not jump to conclusions, Ms. Kincaid. We're not saying that we believe Matthew Childs is a killer. All we're saying is there is a high probability—" The man stopped and tried again. "He fits the criteria—" He started one more time. "He matches some of the criteria.…"

"'*Some* of the criteria'?" She suddenly found the voice that fear had hidden from her. "How much of the criteria does someone have to match before you decide they're a serial killer? Fifty percent? Seventy-five? Ninety-nine and nine-tenths?"

"Calm down, Miz Kincaid." The detective took a shuffling step forward, finally abandoning his post by the door. "Like the doc says, we're not saying Childs is a killer. Just a suspect." He paused, then added, "Among others."

"Others? Like who?" she challenged.

The white-haired man stiffened. "I'm not at liberty to say." His gaze lingered on her for a moment too long and suddenly she realized the implication.

"Me?" She gasped the word. An uncomfortable snake of electricity slithered up her spine. "You're trying to tell me that I'm a suspect, too?"

The detective raised one shoulder in a gesture of uncertainty. "Don't leave town."

Jill elbowed past him as she headed for the door. As if offering a conciliatory bit of information, the doctor called out, "Ms. Kincaid, if it'll make you feel a bit better, there's only been one accepted, documented case of a serial killer who was female."

Jill leveled him with a scorching stare, turned and walked out.

There was only one place she wanted to be right now. With her son. Once she slipped his warm hand in hers and placed a kiss on his soft cheek, she'd be able to sort through everything. Untangle her thoughts. Figure out what to do.

But as she trudged up the stairs to the Pediatric ward because the elevator was unforgivably slow to reach the floor, her mind was consumed with what-if questions.

What if Matthew Childs wasn't the kind, caring individual he seemed to be?

What if he was a killer?

What if he killed Bummpt?

The part of her soul that still ached from the lingering memories of her ex-husband's abuse cried out with a rousing cheer, but she couldn't help but think of the others who had died and those who had been placed in danger—her son and Matthew's sister.

"Bummpt didn't deserve to die," she said aloud, as if trying to override the less generous thoughts that skulked in the shadows of her heart. "No matter how bad…no matter how frustrating he was, he didn't deserve to die." And then there was Danny. He didn't deserve losing a father, even if that father was a card-carrying louse.

As she approached the Peds hallway, she spotted the guard, standing at her son's door.

What about Matthew?

Was he a killer? Or merely a convenient scapegoat? Perhaps it was easier for the police to concentrate on him than to look for the real killer.

Real killer?

She drew a deep breath. What made her so sure Matthew Childs was no killer? Instinct? Intuition? She'd been wrong before…painfully so.

When she entered Danny's room, she was surprised to see her son awake and sitting in Mrs. Flynn's lap. They hovered over something colorful and evidently interesting that he held in his lap.

For a moment, they made a perfect picture—a grandmother and her son, a picture that had no equivalence in the real world. Danny had no loving gray-haired grandmother to make him cookies, to buy him presents for no reason at all, to tell him old embarrassing stories of his parents' childhood.

The woman spoke in a soft voice. "Now wrap the yarn that way, and pull it through…that's perfect, Danny!"

Her son looked up, spotting her, a smile of recognition replacing the one of pride shining in his face.

"Look, Mom!" He held up a tangled ball of red yarn. "I did it myself. Mrs. F. teached me."

She and Mrs. Flynn spoke simultaneously. "'Taught' me." They shared indulgent grins.

"Thank you for watching Danny for me."

The woman gave Danny a hug that he miraculously seemed to like. Usually he kept his demonstrative reactions limited to a small circle of people. The circle had evidently widened by one.

"Danny's a delightful boy. Quick, smart and a real gentleman."

Danny nodded solemnly. "I said 'cuse me when I burped."

Jill swallowed back her gentle rebuke and stepped forward to study the tangle of yarn. "Crocheting?" she guessed.

Mrs. Flynn nodded. "When Danny woke up, he was slightly upset until I showed him the baby blanket I was knitting."

"I wanted to knit, too, but Miz F. said the—" he shuddered as he said the next word "—*needles* were too sharp for me to use. But she showed me how to cro-kay, instead."

"Crochet," Mrs. Flynn corrected with good nature. "Look how well he's done." She reached down into a canvas grocery bag and revealed a long, uneven daisy chain of red yarn. "He's an absolute natural, Miss Kincaid."

Jill walked over and sat on Danny's bed. "And I have a use for some of this already." She pulled back her hair with one hand and used a length of the crocheted yarn to hold a ponytail. "What do you think? It even matches my shirt."

Mrs. Flynn rewarded her with a nod and a smile.

Although Jill wasn't looking for and didn't need the woman's approval, it still made her feel good. After all of the panic and problems she'd faced in the last forty-eight hours, it was nice to be reassured that she was a good mother.

But the most satisfying gesture of reassurance came only a moment later.

Danny abandoned his crocheting and climbed out of Mrs. Flynn's lap and into hers. "I missed you," he said, snuggling into her chest. It was a moment of sheer bliss when she could forget, however momentarily, that their lives were in turmoil.

But her sense of well-being was fleeting.

Danny pulled back and looked at her with almost joyful expectancy. "Did you see Uncle Matt? Is he coming back? Can we go back to his house?"

Uncle Matt.

A couple of extra beats rocked her heart. For the moment, her happy, bright-eyed little boy was back to normal and what seemed to please him the most was the thought of getting back with his Uncle Matt. If there was any chance of danger, any chance that Matthew might be anything other than a kind, good-hearted man, then Jill would take no chances. They'd stay in a hotel until the police said it was okay to go home.

Danny continued on, unaware of her sense of uncertainty. "I want to show Uncle Matt how I can cro...cro...do this stuff. And Mrs. F. says that he has some video games on his computer and a train set in the attic that I can play with. Did you know she lives there, sometimes? She's a keephouser." He looked up with a plaintive gaze. "Mom, when can I leave this place and go back to Uncle Matt's?"

Jill froze.

"Where *is* Uncle Matt? Doesn't he want to see me?"

Mrs. Flynn distracted Danny by handing him a ball of blue yarn and starting a few stitches. Then she hustled Jill out of the room.

"What?" the woman demanded as they stood in the hallway. "Is it Matthew? Is he all right? Is there something you didn't want to say in front of Danny?"

Jill fought to control her panic. "He's with the police. They're questioning him."

Mrs. Flynn paled. "Questioning him? About what?"

Jill glanced at the guard and motioned for Mrs. Flynn to follow her. She didn't want anyone to overhear them, especially the police. "About the m-murders."

"Because of the attack on Carol?"

Jill swallowed hard. "Because they think he may have killed her husband...my ex-husband." Jill had no idea what reaction to expect—a shrill denial, outrage, shock.... But what she didn't expect was laughter.

Mrs. Flynn burst out in a hearty case of giggles. "Matthew Childs? A killer? That has to be the silliest thing I've ever heard. That boy doesn't have a mean bone in his body."

After a moment, Jill realized she liked the sense of surety the woman possessed. "You sound...certain."

She patted Jill on the arm. "Of course I do. I've known Matthew since he was a very small boy." Her smile faded somewhat. "His father and my husband had been very good friends and our families stayed close even after his father's death."

"He…he told me about his father."

"Those pictures on his wall pretty much spell out the whole thing." She glanced off into the distance. "I still have a hard time looking at them. I don't spend much time in that room because of them." Her gaze sharpened and snapped back to Jill. "But Matthew did what he set out to do. He kept badgering the police until they reopened the case. They eventually found the killer and put him behind bars."

"I think the police are talking to him because of what they call his…fascination with crime."

"Fascination?" The woman released a short bark of laughter. "Nonsense. He's an investigative reporter. There's nothing strange or abnormal about that."

Jill had to agree with Mrs. Flynn, but there was a good chance the woman might be thinking with her heart rather than her brain. Yet, if anyone knew Matthew Childs well, it might be his housekeeper. Jill had to push on. "Do you know anything about…profiles?"

Mrs. Flynn turned sideways and tapped her nose. "With a honker like this, I avoid profiles whenever possible."

"Not that type of profile. A criminal one, where they figure out what sort of person a serial killer is likely to be."

The woman's brows knitted. "What about them?"

"Matthew…matches their profile." Jill closed her eyes and held her breath, but she was totally unprepared for the woman's response.

"So?"

Jill opened her eyes and gaped at the woman. Mrs. Flynn seemed quite bright, but evidently the nuances of the situation had eluded her. Jill tried to remember all the criteria the doctor had mentioned which eerily seemed to fit Matthew. "They're looking for a man in his late twenties, early thirties, who probably didn't know the victims. They think he has a fascination with police work and probably suffered some sort of trauma as a child."

Mrs. Flynn made a sweeping gesture at the people in the hallway. "Congratulations. You're in the midst of at least three potential serial killers." She nodded toward the guard. "He told me earlier that his dog died when he was eight. Seems to me he'd match the profile just as well as Matthew would." She pointed down the hallway to an orderly pushing a woman in a wheelchair. "What about him? He's male, the right age, and he probably didn't know the victims, either."

"But they took Matthew away."

Mrs. Flynn shook her head. "It's called cooperating with the police. If they didn't investigate Matthew thoroughly, then I'd be worried. But don't worry. He's one of theirs. They'll treat him right."

Jill crossed her arms. *One of theirs?* "You mean...Matthew's a cop?"

"No, not a cop. A cop's son. That's why he's a crime reporter. They know him, they trust him."

"I thought it was because..."

"Because his father died a violent death and he's been using the police to find his father's killer?" Mrs. Flynn shrugged. "I won't lie and say that it's always been strictly business with him. But revenge isn't the reason why he works on the outskirts of the cop business. It's resolution."

Resolution. That had a healthy ring to it. But one thing still bothered her. "I thought he said his father was a printer."

The woman's soft smile spoke volumes. "He was. When I said Matt was a cop's son, I meant his mother. Mary Margaret, worked for the police, but after Leon died, she couldn't handle it. No wonder she stopped coping. She'd lost her husband and her profession." She paused, looking past Jill's shoulder and down the hallway. "Why don't you ask him about all this?"

Matthew slowly approached them, his jacket thrown over one shoulder. He looked exhausted, frustrated, but definitely not lethal.

However, she'd misjudged people in the past....

Mrs. Flynn crossed her arms in mock sternness. "And where have you been, young man?"

"Getting grilled by Sid Morrison." He drew an imaginary banner in the air. "I can just read the headlines—'Fourth Estate Gets Third Degree.'" Matthew shot them both a tired grin.

Any other time, Jill would have found it attractive, but now? She wasn't sure.

Mrs. Flynn gave him a scathing once-over. "You look like you survived the questioning well enough."

He shrugged. "I came out of it with everything still intact. You know Sid. All bark, no bite."

"So, what did he want to know?"

"Times, dates, alibis." Matthew shook his head as if trying to shake off the memory. "Let's not get into that, right now." He inched toward the door. "How's our little soldier?"

Jill shifted between him and her son's room, suddenly feeling the need to guard her child from all threats, known and unknown. "Danny's...asleep. I don't want to wake—"

A small chirpy voice from inside the room betrayed her. "Uncle Matt? That you?"

Matthew's momentary look of disappointment faded to a tired smile. "Good, he's awake." He took another step toward the room and Jill braced herself, trying to fill the hallway as best as she could, despite the futility of the gesture. She felt her hands tense involuntarily into fists.

"I don't want you to bother him right now. He needs to go back to sleep." Her own voice sounded shrill and ineffective.

But Danny was persistent. "Uncle Matt? I want to show you something cool."

"Just a minute, buddy," Matthew called around Jill. He leaned toward her, lowering his voice. "I promise I won't let him get excited or keep him up long. Just let me—"

Jill pushed him away. "You're not going in there. Understand?"

The guard took note of Jill's demand and moved toward them, only to suddenly return to his station by the door. Jill turned around and saw Mrs. Flynn gesturing to him.

"What's wrong, Jill?"

She turned in time to watch something that looked uncannily like honest confusion fill Matthew's face.

"Is Danny worse? Did he have a relapse? But he sounds all right...." He appealed to Mrs. Flynn. "Did something happen while I was away?"

Jill grabbed the woman's sleeve, hoping she'd help to dissuade Matthew from demanding entrance. Or an explanation. It was more than she could bear at the moment. "You understand, don't you?" she pleaded quietly to the woman.

Mrs. Flynn graced her with a sad smile and shook her head. It would be Jill's responsibility to break the news to him. But before she could speak, the color drained from Matthew's face.

"Wait...you don't—you think I would..." He gaped at her. "You think I killed those people?"

Janet Power   181

move to him. Then it more likely sent them, for Jane spoke
the last few nervously chosen.

"Why don't you go out back, I would..." He
paused as her "Oh, there" forced those just left.

Chapter Thirteen

She blocked the door, a fierce mother tiger, dedicated
to protecting her young from all dangers, real and perceived. But Matthew was no danger and the sooner
she learned that, the better.

He took a step back and raised his hands, hoping
she would read the gesture as an indication of his good
intentions as well as his acknowledgment of her ability
and right to defend her child.

"Uncle Matt," a plaintive voice called from within
the room. "C'mere."

"Just a minute, sport." Matthew's gaze locked with
Jill's steely-eyed one. A myriad of emotions hid behind the wall of strength. "Your mom and I have to
talk."

She started to protest, but stopped. A tremble
coursed through her body and Matthew had a strong
suspicion that rage was more likely the cause rather
than fear. One look at her knotted fists confirmed it.

"Jill," he started, "I'm not—"

"No. You're not." It was a threat, something he
didn't quite expect from her but something he had to
respect. She closed her eyes for a moment, then
opened them, having regained some control and

knocking down a few stones of the wall between them. "Look…it's been a long day. I'm too tired to deal with this right now."

He fought the instinct to step closer, to touch her. Right now, she didn't want to be touched by anyone, especially by him, and he knew it. But the uncertainty, the distrust that hung between them didn't need to remain. In silence, it would fester and grow into misconceptions that might never be resolved. And that was a prospect he couldn't tolerate.

"Don't shut me out, Jill," he said in his softest voice. He pointed past her to the door. "There's a very neat little kid in there who has seen something that no child should. I've been there. I understand it better than anybody."

"You're not a professional."

"No, I'm not. And I don't pretend to be. That's why I called in Oskar. But Danny trusts me and I can tell you that's a rare commodity for any kid to have after going through what he's experienced." He pushed back the cloying inner voice that still demanded that he protect his most intimate secrets, but this was the place, now was the time and Jill was the only person with whom he knew he could share them with. Emotion made his voice uneven. "I grew up, not trusting anyone—my mother, my sister…because they told me everything would be all right." He closed his eyes. "And they lied."

Jill flinched and it took Matthew a second to realize he'd made two mistakes: he'd moved closer to her and he raised his voice. He stepped back.

"Jill," he whispered, "I did not kill Bummpt. After what I went through, what I saw, I couldn't kill anybody." A thousand memories swirled through his mind, images blending in with images, faces merging with faces, all accompanied with momentary flashes of emotion.

Fear, anger, a sense of helplessness, a need for retribution...

His whisper grew hoarse. "When they finally caught the man who murdered my father, there was a big discussion about whether to go for the electric chair or not. I wasn't too sure what good it would do to execute a man who had made a stupid, tragic mistake when he was eighteen—old enough to know better, but young enough to not realize the fragility of life, even his own. He was young, on drugs and desperate. After a couple of years hiding and living with the guilt, he managed to grow up. He got clean, stayed clean and tried to live a relatively decent lifestyle. And then he was caught."

Jill eyed him carefully. "You...you forgave him?"

"Of course not. He killed my father. But killing him wouldn't bring my father back, would it?" He felt blood rush to his face. "But I'm afraid Carol didn't share that line of reasoning."

"That's why you two..."

"That's why we hadn't spoken in six years. I was hoping the book I'm writing might help explain why I thought what I did and help her to understand. I was hoping it would open the door she'd shut between us."

Jill unclenched her fists.

He held out his hand, palm out. "Jill, I promise to you on all that is sacred in my life, on my father's grave, that I'm not a killer. It's simply not in me to kill. I know firsthand."

A pounding electricity flowed through his veins, propelled by his thundering heart. The noises of the hospital faded in the background as the blood rushed through his ears. Every muscle in his body prickled and inside his clenched fists, his palms were damp. Past and present merged for a moment, and he was back in that dark alley, going where a young man bent on a vendetta should never go.

Ah yes...the vendetta. The part he had blithely skipped over as he recited the sanitized version of his story. That's all most people knew...the sanitized version. But the book was going to reveal the true story, attempting to explain how his enlightenment about capital punishment had come at a strangely apt time in his life.

In a dark, deserted inner city alley...

The streetlight had been broken for two weeks, shot out by a passing gunman. Matthew had been quite proud of his ability to hit it from a moving vehicle. It wasn't a technique one readily picked up at a shooting range, but he'd improvised by working with a moving target, instead. It worked in theory and, considering the streetlight, in practice as well.

The police had abandoned the area a month earlier, saying that their quarry had moved on to greener pastures. But Matthew listened to his reporter's instinct that said otherwise.

He knew John Carl Duquette was scared and had lost his streetwise edge after years of life in the artificial safety of the suburbs. The man had lost his contacts and because of that, his ability to meld into the dirty alleys and abandoned buildings of midtown. Despite the thickness of its concealing concrete foliage, the inner city jungle was a deadly place for him. There was no honor among thieves and evidently, no sanctuary, either.

John Carl Duquette, aka The Killer, was in fear of his life from the very people who had taught him many long years ago how to kill.

"The Killer."

Matthew thought of him in no other terms. It was a simplistic name, designed to rob the man of any humanity, any chance to win sympathy or compassion. Tracking a man named Duquette had connotations that Matthew wasn't willing to contemplate. He found it infinitely easier to track down "the Killer" as if he were tracking down some inanimate object.

But the man cowering in the alley wasn't an inanimate object. He was a human being, scared, hurt, lonely and he had a life.

"Please…don't kill me. I have two little girls. And my wife is sick."

"She's dying of lymphatic cancer," Matthew stated flatly. "I know all about your family, Killer. I know all about you. And you know it's all over."

Duquette gasped. "Who are you?"

A long time ago, when Matthew had a sense of humor, he would have growled, "I'm your worst nightmare." But he'd lost what little humor he possessed when they reopened his father's case. Now he was his own worst nightmare.

"My name is Matthew Childs."

"Childs?" The man let out a rattling sigh. "Oh my God…you're his son."

"Leon Childs had two small children, too. And a wife who eventually died of a broken heart. Why shouldn't I kill you? Why shouldn't you and your family suffer the same fate we did?"

In the shadows of the alley, he saw a movement.

Was Duquette arming himself? Preparing to make a stand? Preparing to make a run for it?

Matthew's hand tightened on the gun grip, his finger braced against the trigger.

Duquette rose awkwardly to his feet.

Every nerve in Matthew's body jumped, except for his trigger finger.

"Please…"

Matthew sited on the man's chest.

Duquette held out one hand, but used the other to reach behind his back. "I want to show you…"

Matthew knew what "this" was likely to be. A gun, a knife, a reason for him to kill this bastard and make the world just a bit safer.

"…this."

Duquette held out his wallet.

Matthew spoke, his voice sounding oddly raspy. "You don't have enough money in the world to save yourself, pal."

"Not money," the man said with a sob. He flipped the wallet and it fell open to a faded photograph. Even in the failing light, Matthew could see two little girls in starched dresses trimmed in lace, their sweet smiles frozen forever.

Twins.

Duquette fell to his knees. "Don't hurt them, please."

Matthew's spine stiffened involuntarily. "What?"

"My little girls." Duquette stroked the picture with the tips of his fingers. "Sharleena and Tamlyn. Please don't hurt them. They didn't do anything wrong. I did. I'm the one who shot your father. They're innocent."

Matthew swallowed back his own wave of strong

emotion. "I was innocent, too. They'll have to live with their father's death just like my sister and I did."

He expected Duquette to plead, to beg on bended knee for his life. It had been a scene Matthew had anticipated for over a year as the search for the Killer had heated up. In his dreams, Matthew had pulled the trigger without compunction or hesitation. There would be no second thoughts with a bullet snug in the chamber. Duquette would beg for his life and Matthew would take it away in a deadly flash of light, without a single moment's thought. But nowhere in the dream or the nightmares had Matthew included retribution on innocent children. Of course, he'd spent most of his childhood waiting for the Killer to come back and finish the job, killing the only witness to his crimes. But he took no joy from knowing Duquette thought he had to plead for mercy for his own children's lives.

Matthew straightened to his full height. "I'd never touch your kids. And I'll make sure they're taken care of. But that's more of a chance than you ever gave me."

The milk of human kindness evaporated as an image of his father's bleeding body flashed through his mind. "I heard you argue with my father. I heard the things you said. I heard you threaten my sister's life and mine. I had to live with that threat all of my life, waiting, wondering when you'd strike. But your children won't worry. That's one circle I'm glad to break."

To his surprise, the man lifted his face, revealing a tear-stained smile. "Thank you," he said with what seemed to be genuine joy. "I believe you. Thank you."

Duquette closed his eyes and lifted his head back slightly, affording Matthew a clear shot at his chest.

One bullet in the heart would end his suffering.

One bullet...

One...

MATTHEW FOCUSED ON Jill's face, her look of wariness having slipped away, replaced by the expression of soft strength that he'd begun to think of as uniquely hers. It gave him the impetus to go on.

"I couldn't do it. I couldn't take the life of the man, even though he just confessed to killing my father and I had a gun aimed at him. I would have been no better than him." He started pacing, unable to stay still. "You see...the problem with 'an eye for an eye and a tooth for a tooth' is that it never ends. Would one of his children grow up with a desire for revenge on the man who killed her father? Would my child retaliate? The cycle would be unending. Someone had to stop it. And I did."

He stopped, and took a deliberate step closer to her. This time, she didn't flinch or move away. "Jill, I don't know who has said what to you, but I faced that moment where I had to decide whether I could kill or not. And I found out I couldn't."

Jill searched his face as if she were looking into his mind, reading his thoughts, seeing the unpleasant memories. She swallowed hard, then stepped aside. "Danny wants to show you something."

As he passed by her, she whispered, "Then we need to talk."

AN HOUR LATER, they were back in the hospital cafeteria, nursing sodas with little interest. Oskar and Jeff had shown up and had been pressed into duty as entertainers for Danny who showed no signs of sleepiness. In fact, he was almost manic in his desire to "play." Oskar assured them it wasn't an abnormal reaction, considering what Danny had been through.

Matthew couldn't help but note that Oskar didn't say it was normal, just not abnormal.

Jill toyed with her straw, watching the bubbles in the soda lift it. She probably noticed the double-talk of terminology, too. But it was time for other things.

Time to talk.

He took a fortifying gulp of his drink. "Bummpt's killer knows me."

She jerked and looked up. "What?"

"At least he knows of me." He took another long draw of his tasteless drink. "The killer seems to be getting his inspiration from an article I wrote some time back about the increase of violence in our society and its effect on today's children." The copy of the newspaper clipping felt as if it were burning a hole in his jacket pocket. "You're not alone in your suspicions. Sid Morrison decided I needed to provide him with alibis for all the murders."

She studied his face. "Could you—" she cleared her throat "—did you come up with the alibis?"

It was his turn to play with his drink. "For the most part. I tend to keep pretty good track of my time on the computer. I figure Sid's out checking out all the places where I said I was. But..."

"But what?"

He released a sigh of frustration. "We're talking about times ranging back well over a year ago. People have a way of forgetting who was where. I have receipts and things like that, but who's to say they're my receipts?"

She looked appropriately shocked. "Then you think the lieutenant is going to arrest you?"

Matthew shrugged. "It's a distinct possibility. The best course of action I have is to investigate on my own. Maybe I can turn up what the police haven't. I have a feeling that if I don't take an active part in my own defense, things are likely to get much worse."

"This article you wrote... I don't understand how the killer used it. I know Bummpt wasn't no poster child for peacekeeping, but why did you mention Bummpt in an article about increased violence? And who did you mention that hasn't turned up as a victim, yet?"

Matthew's heart took an extra lurch. They'd been busy concentrating on the previous deaths. No one had mentioned future victims. He pulled the article from his pocket, thankful that he'd coerced Sid into making a copy for him. Smoothing out the folds of the paper, he started reading it again.

Jill shifted her chair closer, right next to him. Her presence was reassuring as well as distracting. As he read, he found it exceedingly difficult to concentrate on the words as he felt a slight pressure against his arm and realized she was leaning against him to get a better view of the paper.

He broke off for a moment to steal a glance at her. She lifted her eyes and where he feared he'd see lingering distrust, he saw acceptance. She reached over and touched his hand.

"I may have a lousy track record when it comes to trusting the wrong people, but my son is the best judge of character I know. Danny trusts you, implicitly."

Matthew closed his eyes and released the breath he'd been holding. Suddenly, he felt a slight pressure on his cheek, an innocent touch that burned just like the most provocative caress. When he opened his eyes, she had turned her attention back to the article.

A kiss? Had she really kissed him?

He tried to read, but he was hopelessly distracted. He stared at the side of her face, wishing he could see more behind the curtain of hair that had fallen forward to veil her features. He used his forefinger to gently pull back the hair and tuck it behind her ear. She shot him a sidelong glance that held a thousand questions.

And questions demanded answers.

Answers. Damn it. That's what he needed to be worried about. Not about the distractions in life, no matter how strong, no matter how enticing. He needed to save his own skin before he could entertain more personal thoughts.

He tried to read the article, to analyze his own words with some sort of detachment. It wasn't a matter of why he wrote what he did, but what someone might read into it. What sort of interpretation, what sort of direction would an unhinged mind find in his words?

What sort of—

She kissed him again. It was short, sweet and full of promises. As she pulled back, she ducked her head, as if embarrassed at the brazenness of her action.

Brazen, hell.

He reached up, gathered her face in his hands and kissed her back. As their lips touched, the first of their unspoken promises was broken. Their timing stank. This was neither the time nor the place to indulge their desires. But desires could be demanding and perhaps in this case, even beneficial. If she trusted him enough to kiss him, then she believed him. As simple as that.

Perhaps now they wouldn't spin their wheels, doubting each other.

But why do you trust her? his voice of doubt prodded. *You know nothing about her.* From his years in the field, he knew that ruthless killers could come in small, pretty packages with wide-eyed stares and innocent smiles.

Who is Jillian Kincaid?

Chapter Fourteen

"I'm not who you think I am," she started. "When I married Bummpt, I was wild, crazy. I drank too much, I smoked too much, and I had some other habits that weren't too healthy."

"Drugs?" Matthew asked softly.

"No, but that's because I was...unbalanced enough without them." She amended her statement quickly. "Not unbalanced like insane, but unprincipled. I did dangerous things without a second thought."

"Was Bummpt one of those dangerous things?"

She nodded. "Very dangerous. But it was probably the best and worst thing that I'd ever done. It was like getting a partner in my self-destruction, but then I started to care for him. And when I realized that what he was doing might jeopardize his life, it made me want to stop him. Instead, I stopped myself." She shifted uncomfortably in her seat. "Can we head back to Danny's room and talk along the way?"

"Sure." Matthew stood up and helped her from her chair.

"Manners." She smiled weakly at him. "I like that. I didn't grow up knowing much about manners."

Matthew shrugged, almost embarrassed by the attention paid to something he considered a natural act. They negotiated a path through the hospital cafeteria and out to the hallway.

"As I was saying, seeing firsthand the life that Bummpt was living and how it affected him, me, the people around us, I started not liking who and what I was. I wanted to grow up. But Bummpt didn't like the idea of that because my growing up meant growing away from him." She wrapped her arms around herself, a gesture Matthew had watched her perform many times when something unpleasant was in the offing.

"His reaction was…volatile and I felt guilty for not being the woman he'd first wanted. I think that's why I stuck around, took his…abuse."

Matthew's arms tightened involuntarily. He was incensed at the thought of Bummpt lifting a hand against Jill.

Or Carol…

A new wave of guilt began to settle across his shoulders. *I should have been in her life…*

"He knew I was going to leave, so one night—" Jill splayed a hand across her stomach "—he arranged for a special little party which included a special additive in my farewell drink." She continued to walk a slow, steady pace as she recounted her tale in a detached voice. "The next morning I woke up with no memory of the night before. But it didn't take long to realize I was pregnant."

Matthew halted in his tracks. "He raped you?"

She looked annoyed that he'd stopped. "Maybe. Or maybe I considered it one last hurrah. I don't remember. Either way, I knew I had to clean up my life, for the baby's sake if nothing else. It drove a bigger wedge between Bummpt and me. He got more violent until one night when I was eight months pregnant. He hit me and I went into premature labor.''

Matthew dropped his head. ''That bastard,'' he said between clenched teeth.

Jill nodded. ''I agree. Luckily, there were no complications and Danny was okay. But when I left the hospital, I didn't go back to Bummpt's house. I filed for a divorce as soon as possible and we went our separate ways.'' She paused. ''As you can see, I got the best end of the deal. I walked away with a beautiful, loving son who will never be like his father. If I work really hard and give him what he needs in life, maybe he'll grow up a kind, smart man with... manners.''

They remained quiet during the rest of the trip back to Danny's room. As Jill started to enter, she paused and turned to Matthew, tears glistening in her eyes. ''I wonder, though... How I can consider myself a good mom when my son is lying in a hospital bed, having nightmares about what he's seen?''

Matthew pulled her back gently. ''Jill, you're a great mom and you're raising a fantastic kid. What happened to him isn't your fault. It's Bummpt's.''

She wiped her tears on the back of her hand. ''We can't be sure. Bummpt may have merely been an innocent victim.'' She snuffled and it turned into an ironic laugh. ''Although I've never used the word *innocent* to describe him, before.''

He reached up and thumbed away the remaining tears. ''Why don't we let the police figure it out.''

''I have a feeling you won't be content sitting back and letting them do all the work.''

He lifted one shoulder. ''I may have to. I'm going to be busy taking care of you and Danny.''

She bristled slightly. "I don't need someone to take care of—"

"Hold it, hold it." He raised his hand, palm out. "Let me try again. I'm going to be busy helping you and Danny take care of yourselves. Okay?"

She mulled over his words, then finally nodded. "Okay."

JILL SPENT THE NIGHT with Danny in the hospital and Oskar and Jeff returned to Matthew's house to pick up some work papers that Jeff had left behind in his rush to tend to Danny's medical emergency. Matthew offered to deliver the papers in the morning, but Jeff insisted he had to have them that night.

Jeff shuffled his feet. "I feel sort of responsible for Danny's asthma attack." He turned to Matthew. "We were building a house of cards and it fell and he got angry at me. That's when he started having trouble breathing."

"Nonsense," Oskar proclaimed. "You didn't cause it. You merely triggered a condition that preexisted. I'm just thankful it occurred in my presence so someone was here who knew what it was and how to deal with it." Oskar scratched his chin in thought. "However, I will say that Danny's mother seems a fairly competent woman. I don't think she would have completely panicked had it happened when she was alone with him."

"Jill's a very smart lady," Matthew offered in her defense, "and a very loving mother."

"Indeed, she seems quite devoted to the boy. But devotion isn't enough in this case. He's unwilling to face his memories on a conscious level and this will continue to trigger subconscious reactions such as the asthma or maybe something worse. The sooner we can force him to remember the sequence of events, the better."

"*Force* him?" The word had several unpleasant connotations associated with it. As a child, Matthew had the opposite problem; he knew exactly what he saw but no one would listen to him.

As if reading Matthew's thoughts, Oskar shook his head. "No, his situation differs from yours, Matt. You were desperate to expose the truth whereas Danny seems desperate to hide it. There's one very good reason why I think he might want to hide the truth."

Matthew knew where the doctor was heading and he didn't like it. "You think his mother did it?"

Oskar clicked open his watch and felt the hands for the time. "I didn't say that. But she is someone that he might feel compelled to protect."

"So you think he's protecting the killer?"

"Perhaps."

"But why?"

Oskar stood. "I'm feeling suddenly fatigued. Can we continue this discussion in the morning?"

Matthew stood as well. "Don't stonewall me, Oskar. Who is he trying to protect?"

The doctor cocked his head, then pursed his lips. "Make a list, Matthew. Who does he love enough to try to protect?"

"Carol? But she didn't do it. She was almost killed herself. You didn't see the cuts on her arms. They were deep, but definitely cuts she got while trying to defend herself."

"And she has no memory of the attack, either?"

"No."

"That's...convenient, don't you think?"

MATTHEW DIDN'T SLEEP that night. Although he made a valiant attempt to rest, bloody images ran through his mind, kick-starting the part of him that hated unsolved problems.

He poured over every article he could find about the victims. He even spent the better part of the night looking for the sixth victim.

By the time the sky turned bloodred with early morning light, he'd narrowed the list down to two possible victims, based merely on the presence of a knife used somewhere at the murder. One victim had been stabbed in a mugging, the other had slit her wrists, committing suicide. Neither case fit the criteria exactly, but if the police in each jurisdiction was holding back key information from the papers, that might account for the lack of connection.

Matthew started his coffee machine, and stretched out on his couch, waiting for it to brew. Three hours later, the doorbell woke him with a start. Stumbling to his feet, he found his way to the front door.

Sid Morrison waited outside, looking mildly impatient.

Matthew opened the door a crack. "Unless you have a warrant, go away. I was sleeping."

Sid smirked. "Warrant? I don't need no stinkin' warrant...." The smirk changed to a grin. "I have something better than a warrant." He motioned to someone beyond Matthew's line of vision.

Jill stepped forward with Danny perched in her arms. Matthew opened the door all the way, confused, but happily so.

"Hi, Uncle Matt. I'm all better!" Danny grinned, then lurched toward him.

Matthew reached out automatically and caught the

child with an expertise that surprised even him. "I didn't expect...I thought you'd call before—"

"Mom, can I have some jammies like Uncle Matt's?"

Matthew looked down, realizing that he stood in his front door, dressed in a pair of faded gym shorts, an old football jersey and a plaid robe which he hadn't belted. He felt his face flush as he tried to close his robe and keep a firm grasp on Danny.

"I offered to take them to a hotel, but Ms. Kincaid insisted on coming here." Sid gave Danny an indulgent smile. "So did the squirt."

"I hope that's all right." Jill stood solemnly on the porch, her look of apparent serenity betrayed only by her interlocked fingers, braided so tightly that her knuckles were almost white. When her gaze locked with Matthew's, a thousand messages flew between them.

Doubt had crumbled away to reveal a pillar of trust. Expectancy flared. She had come on her own free will and evidently with some semblance of cooperation from Sid, which meant neither she nor Matthew was being seriously considered as a suspect.

"Uh...certainly. You and Danny are very welcome to stay as long as you want."

"Forever and ever!" Danny turned in his arms and got a stranglehold on Matthew's neck. "Yay!"

Jill unknotted her fingers. "Now Danny, you remember what I said about going back to school next week. Mrs. Russell would be so sad if I didn't go back to work."

Danny's hug tightened and his voice raised. "No. Don't wanna go to school. I want to stay here."

"Danny..." she admonished.

"No!" He began to cry, kicking away his mother's efforts to take him back.

Not sure what to do, Matthew shot her a weak grin. He adjusted Danny's arm, easing the pressure from his throat "Why don't we go inside and talk there."

Sid threw them a snappy salute. "I'll leave you to deal with the tantrum, yourselves. There'll be a guard outside…for protection." He turned to leave, then paused and called back, "If Danny and the doc come up with anything that looks even remotely interesting, page me. I'm hanging lots of hopes on the little guy. This is one helluva puzzle and I think he's got a key piece." Sid waved to Danny, whose only response was a howl of discontent.

As the door closed, Danny progressed from belligerent to downright ballistic, batting away his mother's efforts to take him and clinging even more fiercely to Matthew.

Matthew tilted his head and made a sympathetic face at Jill. "I've had days like this, too." But he was worried. Who knew if histrionics like this might trigger another asthma attack? He patted Danny on the back, hoping to calm him. "That's okay, sport. We won't worry about that right now, okay? You and me and your momma will go into the living room and see if we can find anything interesting on the TV, okay?"

Calming somewhat, Danny wiped his nose on Matthew's shoulder. "You got videos?" he asked after a prolonged sniff.

"Nothing you'd like. But I bet we can find cartoons on one of the stations."

Danny stuck out his lip and for a moment, Matthew thought it was a precursor to another tantrum. But Danny surprised him by tsk-tsking in disappointment.

"We need to get you some videos so you have sumpin' good to watch all the time. There's a lot of crap on the boob tube."

Jill straightened. "Daniel Robert…what did I say about using those words?"

Danny's protruding lip quivered. "I'm sorry…" He buried his face in Matthew's shoulder and began to cry.

This time when Jill reached for him, Danny didn't fight. He crumpled in her arms and sobbed uncontrollably.

Matthew was at a loss. Even though he knew firsthand how emotions could explode upon you without warning, he'd never seen it occur from such a unique vantage point.

He felt…helpless. And a revelation hit him like a tidal wave, almost forcing the air from his lungs.

I wonder if Mom felt this way, too?

He walked blindly down the hallway, suddenly remembering the constant emotional outbursts he'd had as a child and his mother's slow descent into apathy. Had he driven her there?

Jill shifted her sniffling son and touched Matthew on the shoulder. "What's wrong?"

He stuffed his hands in his pocket. "I think I just got a lesson about the shoe being on the other foot. Even as an adult, I never quite realized how heavy of a burden my mother carried during those years. I was too busy grieving for a missing father to realize she was grieving for a lost husband. Add to that the fact that I'd witnessed my father's death. As horrible as that might have been for me, I've never considered it from her point of view." He pivoted and gazed at Jill and Danny, mesmerized by the sight of mother and child taking comfort from each other.

"I've been watching you interact with Danny and I had started to rebuild some resentment toward my mom for not being as…competent to handle this tragedy as well as you have."

Jill shook her head. "There's a major difference between your mom and me. I'm not grieving a lost husband. I'm sorry Bummpt's de—" she glanced at her snuggling son and changed in midword "—gone. I especially sorry about the violent way he went. But I'm not mourning a mate."

Matthew felt something in him release. It was as if a heavy burden had been lifted from his back. *"The weight of the world,"* his mother had joked during better times. *"Sometimes I think you enjoy carrying the weight of the world on your back."*

"I think you and my mother have…had something in common, too. You love your son and I think my mother loved me. It was the overwhelming sorrow that seemed to blunt the message. But she loved me… loved us."

Carol.

What about Carol? Not only had she lost a husband, she'd lost a child. While he had been busy carrying the weight of the world on his shoulders, he had conveniently left her to cope on her own. Maybe it was his fault that she'd gotten tied up with Bummpt to begin with. If Matthew had been a bit more persistent, a bit more bulletproof to her caustic comments, maybe she wouldn't have fallen into a reportedly loveless marriage with a man with violent tendencies.

Rather than carry the weight of the world, it was about time he looked closer to home.

Home.

As he contemplated the word, an image of Jill and Danny flashed in his head. Why?

Jill managed a small smile. "I think you're on the right track."

Matthew knew she was talking about his revelation about his mother, but there was something almost satisfying about pretending she was talking about being part of a home with him.

Danny seemed to need him. But what about Jill?

She continued, unaware of his thoughts. "Danny's been up since about five, this morning. I think he could use a nap."

Danny turned on the waterworks again. "I don't wanna take a nap." But instead of kicking and screaming, he sobbed into his mother's shoulder. Suddenly he sat up. "Where's Mr. Popster? Where's my Popster?"

Jill rolled her eyes. "Oh Lord…we must have left him at the nurses' station."

Danny collapsed in tears, as if his sole source of support had been cruelly stripped from him. "He's lost. He's alone and he's lost."

Matthew patted the child on the back. "It's okay, sport, I'll call the nurses and make sure they take care of him. Then maybe Jeff and Doctor Oskar can pick him up on their way here."

That seemed to pacify the child to a degree. He calmed down. "But how can I take a nap without Mr. Popster?"

Matthew rummaged around the attic of his mind, trying to remember where any of his old toys might be packed away. A trip into the actual attic would take a couple of dusty hours because the boxes up there weren't labeled and each would have to be opened and examined. Then he remembered two things: he had a stuffed pillow shaped like a football in the hall closet, a legacy from his last trip to the carnival and Danny's army man that he had stumbled over on the living room floor.

"I know just what you need. You get comfortable in your bed and I'll be right there."

Danny sniffed, then burrowed into his mother's shoulder.

She stroked his hair and whispered something to him that seemed to help him make his decision.

"Okay," he muttered.

Jill graced Matthew with a grateful smile, then carried her son toward the guest bedroom.

By the time Matthew had collected the toys and walked back to the guest bedroom, Jill had tucked Danny into the large bed and they were talking softly. Matthew stood in the doorway, trying to neither disturb nor overhear them. He failed on the second count.

"I like Uncle Matt." Danny wiggled deeper into the pillow. "A lot."

"Me, too."

"Can we stay here forever?"

"Forever? No, honey. We have to go back home soon."

He stuck out his lip. "I don't wanna. I wanna stay here."

Jill reached down and kissed his forehead. "You take a nap and we'll discuss it later."

"But I don't wann—"

Matthew stepped into the room, hoping he could forestall the argument with a timely interruption. "Here we go, sport." He placed the ball in Danny's arms. "Now you can be a real sport. Maybe you'll have football dreams." He grinned. "Those are fun." He reached into his pocket and pulled out the army man. "And I found this. You left it here."

Danny reached out slowly and took the plastic soldier, cradling it in him palm as if it were fragile.

"Good night, Danny." Matthew reached down and ruffled the child's hair.

"S'not night," he corrected.

Matthew stifled his laugh. "I stand corrected. Good nap, Danny." He ruffled the child's hair again as if the action and the comment always went hand in hand.

"I'll be in the living room if you need me. I can hear you from there."

Danny seemed suddenly subdued. He placed the army man on the pillow beside him, then turned on his side so he could watch the toy.

Not watch—stare.

He stared at the soldier with such intensity it was as if he expected the toy to animate. Matthew thought the reaction odd, but was pleased that, judging by his grip on the football, Danny seemed to have accepted it as a suitable substitution for Mr. Popster.

Jill and Matthew tiptoed out of the room together and she partially closed Danny's door. Matthew expected the child to protest, but he was so intent on watching his soldier that he raised no objections.

Once in the safety of the hallway, Matthew spoke. "Why was he staring at the army man like that? It was as if he thought it was going to move or something."

Jill waved away the concern. "It's called too many viewings of *Toy Story*. You know…that Disney movie about the adventures of some toys that are alive when children aren't looking? Danny loves that movie. And I guess he's willing to let the plastic soldier take the place of Mr. Popster who usually protects him from the evils in the night."

Matthew nodded. "'From ghoulies and ghosties and long-legged beasties and things that go—'" He stopped short, realizing his faux pas. He started to apologize but Jill shook her head.

"'—bump in the night. Good Lord deliver us,'" she said, finishing the quote. "*'Deliver us,'*" she repeated. Her lips tightened for a moment. "It's not a delivery but a release. Bummpt's death means I've been released from fear. We both have. Danny will never have to fear his father and neither will I. And I can't help but feel guilty about being so relieved."

She stood there, in fragile stoicism. Matthew fought the urge to pull her into his arms into a bear hug. Instead, he took her hand and led her away from her son's room and down the hallway to the living room. He parked her on the couch, helped her swing her feet up, and wrapped her in the afghan Mrs. F. always kept on the end.

"You've spent all your time taking care of Danny. It's time someone took care of you. Stay here. I'll be right back."

In the kitchen, he prepared a mug of hot chocolate and found Mrs. F.'s stash of chocolate chip cookies. On more than one occasion, he'd heard his housekeeper espouse chocolate as a universal antidote. He sure hoped she was right.

When he returned to the living room, Jill's unemotional facade faded when she saw his offerings. She cracked a small smile. "Chocolate."

"Good for what ails you, or so Mrs. F. says." He

set the plate of cookies beside her and made sure she held the mug of cocoa in both hands. "Time for you to be pampered. Would you like me to turn on the stereo and find some music?"

She warmed her face in the steam rising from the mug. "No, thanks. After a night in a noisy hospital, I really like the peace and quiet."

"How about something to read? A book or magazine?"

"I'm fine. It's lovely just like this. Thank you."

Matthew sat down in a large chair, intending to rest, too, but an important thought seized him. "Jeff." He snapped his fingers. "I need to call him and see if he can swing by the hospital and pick up Danny's... whatever that Popster thing is."

Jill looked up from her mug. "Could you ask Dr. McGrath to check his records or whatever and recommend someone for Danny to see when we get back home?"

He stood, trying to belie the momentary sense of panic that hit him at her admission. "You're not leaving...today, are you?"

Jill looked up, almost shyly. "I was hoping we could stay at least one more night. If Danny hasn't remembered anything up to now, what's the chance of him ever doing so? You've seen him. He's getting back to normal."

"What about his reaction at the door? He seemed pretty upset, unnaturally so."

Jill shook her head. "What we saw earlier was a run-of-the-mill temper tantrum, exactly how I'd expect a cranky four-year-old to act who has misplaced his favorite toy. It's time to go back, time to try to reclaim our lives. Danny needs his normal four-year-old's world with all his toys, his friends. I can't take any more time off from work. The more distance we put between ourselves and this…tragedy, the better.''

How could he make her understand that the word *normal* had lost its definition in Danny's world? And it wouldn't get better until the child learned or was taught how to deal with having experienced a very abnormal set of circumstances. And then there was the issue of his safety.…

''May I?'' Matthew gestured for permission to sit on the couch and she shifted over. He sat, trying to come up with the right words to sway her. ''I think you have several things to consider—there's Danny's emotional health and then there's his safety, as well. If you stay in town, Sid's going to make sure you have security, but once you get out of his jurisdiction, it's going to be more difficult to guarantee your protection. You might have to give up a normal world for a while, but what you'll get in return is a safe one.''

Logic was a wonderful thing. It was such a useful way to cover the real content of a message. *Safety, protection*—those were good buzzwords to use. Very accurate ones, too. Danny's safety was paramount and the child would truly be given better protection here rather than in another city. After all, he was a possible material witness.

But Matthew also listened to the little voice in the back of his head that said, *Don't let Jill go. Don't let this one slip away.*

He felt himself blush and he turned his head so she couldn't see his plainly visible reaction. ''You know you and Danny are welcome here for as long as you want.'' He cleared his throat self-consciously. ''I better go make that call.''

Jill reached out and touched his arm. "Don't... don't go." Her hand tingled as she felt the warmth emanate through the sleeve of his robe. "Yesterday...we played Ping-Pong all day long. I doubted you and you doubted me." She pulled him slightly toward her, almost afraid that if she didn't hold on, he might duck away. "But now that those doubts have been put to rest, I just wanted to say..."

She kissed him on his bristled cheek, then pulled back, shocked.

It wasn't supposed to be like that. It was supposed to be a chaste kiss on the cheek in thanks for being a Good Samaritan and being kind to her son.

It was supposed to be simple.

But it wasn't.

It was...exhilarating. Exciting. Stimulating. Oh yes, quite stimulating—right down to her toes that were still curled from the electricity that flowed through her.

But it was a one-sided reaction. All he did was provide one cheek; her imagination provided the rest. Her great powers of creativity had supplied all the heightened reactions, crediting him with a response that her own body had created on its—

Suddenly, she found herself in his arms, her willing lips pressed to his. Every thought vanished from her brain. She couldn't tell which way was up or down, nor did she care. She dug her nails in his arm, not as an act of possession but because every muscle in her body went haywire.

This passion was no mere figment of her imagination. It was real—as real as the breath she could not catch, as real as the hand that tangled in her hair, as real as the lips that were driving her crazy with their sweet fierceness.

If she'd ever been with another man, she couldn't remember it. All she knew was what she was feeling at the moment. The sheer elegance of ecstasy, the superb orchestration of two desires that met in perfect harmony.

He wanted. She wanted.

They wanted together.

She made the first move, tugging at the belt of his robe. *Be bold,* her inner voice told her. *Let him know exactly what you want.*

They spoke simultaneously.

"I want you."

"We can't do this."

His words caught her by surprise and she pulled back. "What?"

He braced one arm against the couch, his tousled head hanging low as if the effort of halting himself had been painful.

"You don't want to..."

He raised his head, revealing eyes that shined with unquenchable desire. "More than you'll ever know." He drew a deep breath. "But Danny..." He pointed to the hallway. "Danny's in there."

She stroked his cheek, finding the roughness almost erotic. "Parents have been making love with their children next door for years."

He swallowed hard. "Yeah...it's called making siblings." He looked up with something close to pain filling his eyes. "I don't have anything." He turned, falling back against her, and released a strangled laugh. "No condom in my bedside table. No condom in my wallet. No protection at all. It's been a...dry year."

Jill tried not to laugh, but she couldn't help it. Then, inspired, she glanced broadly at the front door.

Matthew followed her gaze, then his eyes widened. "Aw c'mon, Jill. A man has his pride. I can't call the guard over and ask him if he's carrying."

She shrugged.

A moment later, Matthew had the front door open, calling the guard over from his station.

Chapter Fifteen

"I feel…almost domestic." Matthew stood behind Jill as she rinsed off their dishes in the sink. He put his arms around her waist and nibbled her ear.

"I'm still hungry," she complained.

"For what?" He began nuzzling her neck, hoping he'd interpreted her appetite correctly.

"For…" She paused, pivoted in the circle of his arms, then graced him with a grin. "For more of those chocolate chip cookies." A gleam twinkled in her eyes. "Where are they?"

He clucked his tongue. "They're Mrs. F.'s secret stash and if you eat them all, she'll get mad."

Jill ducked out his embrace and waved away his concern. "She'll understand. Believe me, she'll understand." She started rooting in the canisters on the counter. "Hmm…flour, sugar—" She stopped. "How did this get here?" She turned around, cradling a slightly sugar-encrusted plastic soldier in her hand. "I thought Danny only had one army man."

Matthew examined the toy carefully. "I thought so, too. I remember him telling Oskar it was a communications officer. But this guy has a bazooka." He thought hard for a moment. "And now that I think about it, the one I gave him in the bed was throwing a hand grenade.''

"Mr. Popster," Jill said knowingly. "He's actually a pajama bag. He has a pocket on his tummy that holds things. I bet Danny had them hidden in there."

"Mr. Popster." Matthew snapped his finger. "I haven't called Jeff about going by the hospital." He grabbed the kitchen wall phone and began to dial. As he waited for someone to answer, an incongruity hit him. "But how did Danny get the toy in the sugar canister?"

Before Jill could answer, Jeff answered the phone. When Matthew explained their predicament, Jeff laughed.

"I know exactly how the kid feels. When I was two, Dad said I had a blanket that went with me everywhere. I'll be glad to play toy delivery man. Only trouble is, Dad can't come today. He's not feeling well and the doctor wants him to take it easy. It's nothing terrible—he's just overdone it the last couple of days."

Matthew covered the mouthpiece. "Oskar can't come because he doesn't feel well. Nothing serious. But Jeff can get the toy. Do you want to ask Oskar to send along some names of good child psychologists in Lexington?"

She nodded. "If he wouldn't mind. But if he's not feeling well enough, we can get the names another day."

"Is Jill there?"

Matthew uncovered the receiver. "Yeah, for the moment. Listen, if Oskar's feeling up to it, could he make some recommendations for a suitable psychologist for Danny in Lexington?"

"I'll ask. She's not going home any time soon, is she?"

"Huh? What?" Matthew's attention was drawn suddenly to Jill. She'd pulled out one of the stools from beneath the kitchen counter and perched on it. The robe she wore—his robe—parted slightly to reveal her bare legs. She followed his gaze and looked down, realizing why he was grinning like an idiot. Wiggling her toes, she pulled the robe closed and shot him an abashed grin.

"Matt? Buddy, you there?"

Matthew suddenly remembered the receiver in his hand. "What, Jeff?"

"I asked if Jill was going home soon."

Matthew gazed at Jill, hoping she'd respond to his look of puppy-dog expectancy. She didn't.

"I hope not, old friend. I certainly hope not."

To THEIR SURPRISE, Danny remained asleep for the entire morning, allowing them time to explore the non-physical side of their new relationship. After Jill called the hospital to make sure Danny's toy was safe until it could be picked up, they talked about everything...except the murders.

They compared childhood tales, high school hijinks, first job stories. If he'd been tasked to invent her life, Matthew wouldn't have gotten anything right. He would have given her a middle-class upbringing, a comfortable berth between siblings, a college education. Instead, he found she'd been orphaned at eight and bounced through the foster care system because she wasn't a cute, adoptable baby, but a stringy-haired tomboy with an attitude. At eighteen, she was turned loose and in her own words, loose she remained.

"I was such a wreck," she admitted. "I'd been turned loose into society without learning any rules about how to cope. I had my high school diploma, but no hopes for college. You needed parents to bankroll that. So I took stupid, meaningless jobs and lost them. I drank too much, smoked too much and did all the things that good girls weren't supposed to do. Of course, I didn't know what good girls did and didn't do. I had institutionalized morals and ethics—you're told what you're supposed to do, but you never quite see it in practice because your exposure to the world is dominated by your peers, who don't know any more than you do." A wistful look crossed her face. "I would have given my right arm for parents."

"Which set did you want? June and Ward from 'Leave it to Beaver' or Mike and Carol from 'The Brady Bunch'?"

She colored quickly. "Actually, I always wanted parents like the Cunninghams on 'Happy Days.' They made mistakes, their kids made mistakes, but somehow, you always knew they loved each other. TV parents... I guess that's silly, eh?"

He shook his head. "Nope. I can remember watching reruns of 'The Big Valley' and wishing my mom could have been a strong woman like Barbara Stanwyck, running a successful ranch, taking care of her children. After Dad died, Mom gave up her career. She simply couldn't take the responsibility."

"Of being a cop?"

He nodded. "Too intense after what she'd been through. She went to work part-time in a beauty salon, which took all her attention. We were left pretty much on our own."

That was an understatement. They were left completely on their own. He'd lost his father physically at six and his mother mentally soon after that. Of course, she still walked around a functional human being, cutting and setting hair, but she wasn't much use to them as a mother. Overwhelming grief had robbed her of her career and the ability to care for children and they ended up caring for her.

Carol tried to play the mother role, but it was too much for her to handle. When she turned eighteen, she ran away from home to party in greener pastures. In fact, Jill and Carol seemed have had a lot in common. The big difference being that Jill had grown up.

But maybe Carol could, too, now that Bummpt was out of her life.

"Do you really think you would have been different if you'd had parents?"

She shrugged. "I don't know. I barely remember my own parents and what I do remember isn't all that wonderful. Maybe I was better off without them. Who knows? All I know is that Danny will never have to go through what I went through." A new light flared in her eyes. "And I appreciate all you've done to help him find a way to deal with what he saw. I wouldn't have known what to do. Thanks. Now I just hope…" Her voice trailed off.

"Don't worry. He's going to be fine. Sid's working hard on the case and Oskar will do whatever he can, too. Between the lot of us, we're going to figure this thing out."

"I'd like to help more. I knew Bummpt better than anybody else."

"You want to look at everything I have on it so far? I spent most of the night collecting data from the newspaper and doing some research into each of the victims.''

''Let's do it.''

Once in Matthew's office, Jill tried not to pay attention to the pictures on the wall. Even though she understood their function in his life, they were still disturbing in their own right.

''My article seemed to have inspired four of the murders, Bummpt, Chandler and the McCreedy brothers. But not the first one, Phoebe Robinson. And evidently they've discovered another victim although they won't tell me anything about the case other than the fact the victim is black.''

''White, black, male, female…'' She shivered in spite of herself. ''What you're saying is that anybody can become one of his victims.''

Matthew tapped the printout on his desk, one which had been covered in color-coded highlights, cramped notes and on the margins, decorated with several doodles. ''But serial killers don't usually change their pattern. Usually they go for the same type of victim—young males or young females, some sort of consistency in how they select their victim. So far, we have in chronological order, a female celebrity with a reputation as a good person, a successful businessman, also with a good reputation, two racers with money but a slimy reputation.…''

''And then there's Bummpt. He was slimy and a spendthrift as well, even though he didn't make as much money as his peers due to bad contract negotiations.''

Matthew raised his eyebrows. ''But only someone who knew him beyond his radio persona might be aware of his real financial situation. On the radio, I hear he sounds as if he's rolling in the dough.''

"His radio station didn't pay his FCC fines, he did. Another bad codicil in his contract. There were several occasions when I didn't get either the monthly child support check or alimony because he cussed a blue streak on the air and the FCC ate up his paycheck. Sometimes, I think he did it on purpose, just so I didn't get the money.'' Jill realized belatedly how her words sounded. She managed a half smile. "Guess I sound like a bitter ex-wife, eh?'' She drew a deep breath. "So money or at least the appearance of it seems to be a continuing factor. Do you think the killer profitted monetarily from the killings?''

Matthew glanced at the papers strewn across his desk. "I hadn't thought about that. But since there seems to be no personal connection between these people, I doubt any one person stood to inherit from them all.''

Jill stared the articles, scanning them, looking for the key that drew them all together in a pattern beyond his article.

"Let's see…Miss Robinson didn't have children, Mr. Chandler did, Bummpt did and the McCreedys, didn't.''

"Correction.'' Matthew reached under a stack of papers and pulled out one. "No legitimate children. I've found at least six different articles concerning paternity suits being brought against the brothers.''

Jill felt her heart start to pound. "And Miss Robinson entertained children. Children,'' she repeated in a whisper. "All of them deal with the welfare of children.''

Matthew scrambled through the pile topped with her

name and pulled out a printout. He ran his finger down the words, searching for something. Jill craned her neck to see as well, straining to read upside down.

Here!'' He stabbed the paper with his finger. He read aloud, '''Although Miss Robinson had no children of her own, she spent the last twenty years founding and funding an organization called For the Good of the Children which raised the plight of orphaned children in war-torn countries. In 1993, she received the Fellows Club Humanitarian Award for her efforts to bring food and supplies into—''' He stopped. ''You're right. Children.'' He skipped down several paragraphs. '''Her personal fortune, estimated around $125 million will go to her charity, and children around the world will benefit from her kind and generous spirit.'''

''A hundred and twenty-five million dollars?'' Jill let out a low whistle. ''That's a lot of food and supplies. Wait! Do you think they meant medical supplies? Chandler had a medical supply warehouse. Is that a connection?''

Matthew nodded. ''Very possibly.'' He grabbed a blank piece of paper and wrote, ''Did children's charity use Robinson money to buy supplies from Chandler?''

''When Chandler died, who got his money?''

''That's the first place where the police look. I called the paper and had a friend nose around. He said it was standard surviving spouse stuff. We're not talking a great deal of money. They lived comfortably and were raising three seemingly normal kids. One was in college and another still in high school at the time. No one can come up with a motive for suicide. That makes the murder angle even stronger.''

"Then his children didn't really benefit from their father's death."

Matthew shook his head. "Not that I can see."

Jill closed her eyes, trying to refine her own thoughts. *For the Good of the Children.* "What about the McCreedy brothers? Who benefitted from their deaths?"

Matthew leaned back in his seat. "Lots of people. Their racing opponents, their pit crew who were paid a pittance—" he grinned weakly at his pun "—and the fathers of every nubile young thing that haunted the tracks." Matthew sprang forward in his chair. "Of course...the children." He thumbed through his research pile concerning the McCreedys. "The six paternity suits may simply be the only ones that reach the courts. Reportedly, their manager had paid off that many girls or more who had gotten pregnant because of one of the brothers."

"So...by eliminating them, you've stopped a reckless source of unsupported, fatherless children in the world. For the Good of the Children..." Jill found herself on her feet, pacing the office. "It all makes sense. These deaths benefitted children in one way or the other. Money from Miss Robinson, the elimination of unfit men who took no responsibility for the pregnancies they caused. And Bummpt? No more impressionable youth getting the wrong message from him. He won't teach them his own brand of prejudice against any and everyone who wasn't exactly like him. It all makes sense to me."

Matthew stayed in his chair, drumming the desk with his fingers. "But what about Chandler? He didn't have lots of money and everything I've found about him suggested he was a good man and a good father."

Jill stood in the middle of the room, her eyes closed. It was a trick she'd learned when she had to escape from Bummpt's verbal tirades and find solace within herself. But this time, she simply wanted to go to that safe place to reorganize her thoughts.

Chandler handled hospital supplies. Not medicines, but all the other things that a hospital used—rubber tubes, bedpans, syringes…

Syringes.

Needles.

Danny was scared of needles, lots of children were.

Danny had been too scared to watch the animated movie Phoebe Robinson had voiced.

Danny was scared of…thunder and lightning.

And things that went bump in the night…

"Fears" she said in a hoarse voice. "The killer is killing all the things he feared as a child." She opened her eyes to discover Matthew, staring at her, his face slack in shock. "Phoebe Robinson played a standard role in fairy tales, the evil queen, in this case, Queen Evila, a totally despicable character who hated children and tried to eliminate them from her kingdom. Danny and I tried to watch the movie but it was too scary for him. I understood that fear completely. I can remember getting just as scared the first time I saw *Sleeping Beauty*. The evil queen in that one haunted my dreams for years afterward."

She walked over the Matthew's desk and placed her hand on the stack of papers concerning the Mc-Creedys. "Vernon and Billy McCreedy. Also known as 'Thunder and Lightning.' All children have been frightened by thunder and lightning at one time or the other in their lives. Danny included." She shifted her hand to the next pile—Nelson Chandler.

"Danny will tell you himself, it's not the doctors he fears, it's the nurses. They're the ones with the needles, who give the shots. But short of killing all the nurses, how do you eliminate the threat?"

Matthew inhaled sharply. "Stop the needles at their source— kill the man who supplies them.

"Exactly. And then there's Bummpt." She started to put her hand on the stack of articles about him, but she couldn't bring herself to touch them. "You said it yourself. He represented all the terrible things that hide in the shadows of the night, all the scary things that go bump in the night."

She dropped in the nearest chair, feeling suddenly boneless from the effort of revelation.

"Childhood fears," she said, her voice remarkably steady. "He's killing his childhood fears."

Chapter Sixteen

"But why childhood fears?" Matthew glanced at the papers scattered across his desk. "We outgrow them."

"Some people don't. A girl I work with is still deathly afraid of thunderstorms. She's never conquered those fears. As far as that goes, I'm not too fond of getting injections, either, even if I know the medicine inside will make me feel better or keep me from getting sick. I still have that little flutter of panic when I see a syringe coming." Her face darkened. "And don't both of us fear still being abandoned because in some ways we were as children?"

Matthew remained silent and she knew she'd hit a sensitive spot. At least his reaction to his "abandonment" had been not to fall into the cycle of single-minded grief that had robbed his mother of her sense of responsibility.

"We've both had some rough times in our lives. But look at Danny. When push came to shove, literally, you stood up for your child and for yourself. You're a great mother, Jill, and Danny's a wonderful kid."

Danny.

Just the thought of him always made her smile and

here she sat, in the midst of a murder investigation, grinning like an idiot. "You know he's going to wake up hungry and cranky and totally impossible. He doesn't usually take morning naps."

Matthew looked at his watch. "It's not morning anymore. It's late afternoon. Almost five. "

"Really?" She winced, not realizing she'd lost track of time so badly. "Then he's going to be even more impossible. I better wake him up and let him get his crankiness out of his system so he'll eventually go back to bed tonight at a decent hour. If I don't we'll be up at midnight with him and I'm too tired for that."

The phone rang and an instant later, they heard Danny crying. Matthew slapped his forehead with the palm of his hand. "Damn it, I forgot to turn off the ringer on the phone in his room. Sorry."

Jill stood and stretched. "He needed to get up anyway. If anything, now it's not mean old momma's fault but the mean old phone's." She headed off toward the guest room.

Matthew picked up the phone. "Hello?"

"It's me. I got the toy—boy, what an ugly thing— but I don't think I can get there until seven. You think the little spud will survive until then?"

"He'll have to. Thanks Jeff, we really appreciate it."

"We? Oooh…don't we sound positively domesticated. Got a collar and a leash, yet?"

"Knock it off, Jeff. I meant Danny and me."

"Okay, okay…just turn on some lights for me and if you have a rent-a-watchdog out there, let him know I'm coming so he won't fire shots into the shadows."

"Done." A howl pierced the air.

"Sounds like the kid's in rare form. You're not telling me you'd miss that around the house, are you?"

It hit Matthew hard, and right in the gut. Would he miss Danny? Damn straight, he would. Danny had brought out instincts that Matthew never dreamed he possessed. He'd never seen himself as father material, but with Danny around, the idea of paternity had crept from nonexistence to a remote possibility to a potential future for him.

"You don't know how much I'll miss Danny when he goes. No idea at all."

"Sheesh. You watch out. Women use their kids like fishhooks, snaring you and reeling you in."

"Goodbye, Jeff," Matthew said pointedly, wanting an end put to this conversation.

"I get the message.... Later." He hung up.

Matthew pushed Jeff's taunts to the back of his mind as he followed the sounds of the banshee named Danny to the living room.

Danny was in a foul mood and made sure everyone knew it. He was hungry, but Uncle Matt didn't have the right type of cereal. When Danny found the last half of a cookie, he wailed about not getting any. Finally he deigned to eat a hot dog and ended up playing with it, rather than eating it. After his so-called meal, he bounced from one distraction to another, unable to concentrate for more than a few moments before bursting out in tears.

Matthew had found his mother's old rocker in the basement and hauled it up to the living room, hoping that it could solve Danny's need for constant motion. Jill rocked him. Uncle Matt rocked him. Danny even rocked himself.

But nothing worked.

Matthew even braved the attic, looking for anything remotely toylike, knowing there was a train set up there, somewhere, but the moment he stepped out of Danny's line of vision, the wailing started again. They ended up all sitting on the couch together, trying to watch television. But Danny had the remote control which meant they were watching the channels flip to his running, but repetitive commentary.

"That scares me."

Flip.

"That scares me."

Flip.

Jill covered her eyes with her arm. "If I survive this, it'll be a miracle."

Matthew picked up Danny and plopped him in his lap, gently wrestling the remote control away. "Tell me about the things that scare you, Danny."

"Scary things."

"Like what?"

Danny pouted. "Loud things."

Matthew pointed to the television. "Like the TV?"

Danny shook his head. "No, like thunder."

Jill uncovered her eyes and shot Matthew a look that said, *Go with that.*

"And lightning?"

Danny rolled his eyes. "Lightning is the light. Thunder is the noise. Boy, Uncle Matt, don't you know anything?"

"What else?"

He wrinkled his nose. "Doctors. Except for Dr. Oskar. He says he never gives shots. I like that kind of doctor."

Jill straightened up. "See? Needles," she mouthed.

"What else?"

Danny pursed his lips. "Santa Claus."

Matthew didn't think he heard right. "Santa Claus? You mean 'Ho, Ho, Ho' and eight tiny reindeer Santa Claus?"

Danny made a face. "The one at the department store. He had bad breath and no face and he didn't know my name."

"No face?"

Jill leaned over. "The department store Santa had a very bushy beard that covered almost all of his face. It was almost like someone wearing a mask and Danny hates it when he can't see their faces."

"Yeah. I didn't like that Santa and I didn't like the clown at the circus and I didn't like—"

Clowns. Where had he run into a reference to a clown? He closed his eyes and thought back, hearing Sid's voice ring in his ear. *No anonymous calls to the city desk about this clown, okay?*

Matthew thought Sid had been making a comment about the murderer, but maybe, just maybe it had been a veiled reference to the sixth victim. A clown. Did he remember anything about a clown who had died?

"Excuse me for a moment." Matthew rose from the couch and headed back to his office at a fast clip. It only took a few moments to tap into the newspaper database and only a couple of minutes to search the archives.

Then the article filled the monitor.

CONVICTED MOLESTER FOUND DEAD

Regis McCamman, a convicted child molester was found dead today in a downtown alley. McCamman, 36, violated parole in 1996 when he fled Ohio where he had served two terms for child molestation and three counts of unlawful carnal knowledge of a minor.

Officials said McCamman joined the Peach Pit Circus in nearby Pennsylvania and had been traveling with them for the past year, working first as a stagehand and then as Cuckoo the Clown. Police report that there had been a string of unsolved molestation cases that followed the circus's itinerary and they believe McCamman was the culprit.

McCamman suffered fatal knife wounds to the chest in what the police believe was a mugging which turned violent. An investigation is pending.

MATTHEW LOOKED AT the date, March 2, 1998. That meant the murder occurred after the McCreedys but before Bummpt. Matthew pulled up his calendar and work log.

The day was blank.

What had he done? Where had he been? Sid Morrison would want to know.

"Well?" Jill stood in the doorway.

"March 2. Cuckoo the Clown from a small traveling circus. He was a convicted child molester on the lam."

A tremor rocked her. "A child molester hiding out as a clown? That's sick. He's sick."

"Well, he's dead now. Only Sid can verify if the same knife was used in this case, but I'd bet the house it was." He stood and walked over to her, enveloping her in a hug. "But think about this pattern—no harm comes to the children. In fact, in each case, there's some sort of direct or indirect benefit for children. Money to a children's charity, no more needles, stopping someone from carelessly conceiving unwanted children…''

Neither one of them were willing to say "stopping things that go bump in the night." He hugged her instead. "I don't think Danny's in danger because he's a child. He's a member of the group the killer is trying to protect."

"You think so?"

He tightened his embrace. "I really think so."

Suddenly, he felt something tugging at his pants leg. "You're hugging Momma."

Matthew looked down. "You're right, sport. I'm hugging your momma."

"Do you kiss her, too?"

Matthew shot Jill a panicked look. *What do I say?* She was no help, her only answer a slightly amused shrug.

"Yes, Danny, I do kiss her." And Matthew proceeded to demonstrate. It wasn't as long or as deep a kiss as he would have liked, but it served as a good punctuation mark to his statement.

Danny seemed content for the first time that day. "Oh, good." He trotted back down the hallway. "Now you'll get married," he said in a matter-of-fact voice.

They broke apart. *Married?*

They stared at each other. *Married?*

"I'm not ready for that," they said simultaneously. A moment later, they both released identical sighs of relief.

Jill busied herself, straightening her borrowed sweatshirt. "I can't afford to stay away from work for more than a few days."

Matthew ran his hand through his hair. "And I have the book to finish."

Danny leaned in from the living room into the hallway, only his head visible. "Can we have babies, too?"

Both Matthew and Jill started toward him, speaking in unison. "Now, Danny..."

IT WAS WHEN Danny finally accepted the fact that kissing didn't mean marriage and babies that he remembered his Mr. Popster was missing. But luckily, the doorbell rang. Playing to a sense of precaution, Jill hustled the child back to the master bathroom and Matthew answered the door by himself.

There he found the police guard, awkwardly cradling the missing toy. The man pointed over his shoulder. "The gentleman in the car said you were expecting this. And he said, next time, please turn on the lights."

"Thanks." Matthew retrieved Mr. Popster and locked the door behind the guard. Turning around, he retraced his steps back to their cautionary hiding place. "Coast is clear."

Jill opened the door and Danny rushed out, only to screech to a halt at the sight of his beloved toy.

"Mr. Popster!" He snatched the stuffed creature and in a bounding jump, landed in the middle of Matthew's bed. "I missed you! Were you a good boy?" Danny turned the toy over, unzipped a hidden pocket and pulled out a toy soldier. "Did Captain Green come protect you, too?"

Jill sat down on the bed and held out her hand. "Can I see him for a moment, Danny?" The child dutifully handed over the plastic soldier. She examined it closely and even Matthew could see the figure had a radio slung on his back. "How many of these army men do you have, Danny?"

He took the toy back. "I have one and Uncle Matt has one."

Jill glanced back at Matthew, who stood at the end of the bed.

Matthew raised his hands, perplexed. "I do?"

"Sure. You let him sleep with me when I took my nap. Him and the football."

"I thought that was yours. You sure you didn't have three of them? We found one in the kitchen."

Danny hugged Mr. Popster with ferocity. "Nope. Just Captain Green. He's here to protect me from the bogeyman."

Jill grew rigid. "The bogeyman? Who's the bogeyman?"

Danny's lip began to tremble. "The guy that killed Daddy. Captain Green guarded me from the bogeyman."

Jill relaxed somewhat. "Your toy guarded you?"

Danny shook his head. "No, Captain Green protected me. He left the army man to report back. See? He has a radio. If there was any trouble, he'd call Captain Green and he'd come an' save me."

Jill reached back for Matthew and he stepped closer, giving her a reassuring pat on the arm. She turned around, her hand covering her mouth as if trying to hold in her tumultuous emotions. Matthew sat down beside her, placing a comforting arm around her shoulders.

"Sport, did you actually meet this Captain Green?"

Danny fiddled with his toy and nodded.

"Was he tall like me?"

Danny nodded again.

"What did he have on?"

The child made a face. "Army stuff. Green splotchy clothes."

"Camouflage," Matthew explained to Danny. "What did he tell you?"

Danny made Mr. Popster spin in a circle. "He said there was a bad man outside and he was going to 'tect me from him. He said to hide and not come out until it was safe." Then without batting an eyelash, Danny tossed Mr. Popster across the room. The creature landed in a heap on the floor.

"I want ice cream," Danny demanded with a howl. "I want ice cream right now." With each repetition, he grew more uncontrollable, more hysterical, flailing and screaming.

Jill grabbed her son and pull him into a tight embrace as much to protect him from himself as well as to console him with her presence.

Danny had survived a face-to-face meeting with a killer. Was this a deliberate action or a mistake that needed to be corrected?

Matthew stood. "I'm going into the other room to call Sid and tell him what Danny said." He strode across the room, but by the time he reached the door, the room plunged in darkness.

Danny howled, but Jill hushed him.

Matthew tried the light switch. Nothing happened. "There's a phone on the bedside table. Is it working?"

He heard a fumbling sound, then Jill's terse answer. "No."

His heart started pounding. "Get back in the bath—" No, they'd already revealed that hiding place when the guard came to the door. Anyone with a brain

could have watched how the lights came on and followed his path through the house back to Jill and
Danny's hiding place.

"No, come with me."

The room was pitch-black so he could rely only on
his hearing to tell that the creaking sound was innocuous, that it came from the bed where Jill rose, probably with her son in her arms.

"Is the bogeyman back?" Danny asked in an un-
characteristic whisper.

Matthew could lie to him and say this was all a
game, but the child, having gone through what he had,
deserved the truth, however unpalatable. "I don't
know, Danny. I want to be careful, though, in case it
is. Can you be real quiet?"

Danny sniffed. "Okay."

Jill bumped against Matthew and he grabbed her
arm. "Follow me."

They inched down the hallway, Matthew feeling for
the door frames that marked the guest bedroom, the
linen closet and the bathroom. "Go in here," he whispered next to her ear, "and lock the door behind you.
If you hear me yell anything but 'The coast is clear,'
that means I know someone's in the house with us. I
want you to crawl out the window and go next door
for help. Got it? Nothing but 'The coast is clear.'"

"Why don't we escape now?"

"Because he might still be outside. Now go." He
pushed her toward the open door, remaining in his spot
until he heard the door lock click like a rifle shot
through the dark, quiet house.

Matthew inched forward, straining to hear other
noises, to categorize them as harmless or potentially
lethal. He paused by his office door. Was someone in

there? He listened carefully. No. The sounds he was hearing came from the kitchen.

Where was that damn policeman who was supposed to be guarding them? An image flashed in his head of a prone figure, coldcocked by the bogeyman. Or should he call him Captain Green?

Matthew dropped to his hands and knees and crawled into his office. He had no real weapons around the house, short of tools in the garage and sharp utensils in the kitchen. He crawled around the edge of his desk and wedged himself beneath. He pressed up against something warm. Inspiration flowed through his veins. His computer's backup power supply. If he could find the plug to his desk lamp, he could lure the man into the office, then blind him temporarily, giving himself opportunity to attack the man while he was confused.

He rooted around, quietly disconnecting the power unit from the computer, and figuring which of the maze of cord belonged to the lamp. That done, he plugged in the lamp, trying to quickly figure out the logistics of his trap. Grasping along the top of the desk, he found the chunk of furnace glass that he used as a paperweight. It was the size of a baseball and quite possibly a formidable weapon.

A crash in the kitchen made him jump, almost dropping the paperweight.

"Oh, dear..."

Matthew stiffened.

"Something went bump in the night...."

The growling voice, although obviously disguised, still sounded vaguely familiar.

"Or was it some*one* who bumped. Bumped the

Bummpt and all those who dared to shatter the dreams of sleeping children. I did it, Mattie.''

Matthew froze. He recognized the voice.

"Jeff?"

Chapter Seventeen

"You can call me that, although I prefer my real name." Jeff was closer, maybe as close as the hallway. A dim light formed out there, growing brighter.

"Your real name? It's Jeffrey." He thought for moment. "Jeffrey Richard."

"That's his name. My name is Jack. I named myself. Jack, the keeper of all truths."

The dim light in the hallway congealed to a beam, probably from a flashlight.

"What do want with me...Jack?"

"You, Matt, my boy? Nothing. You'll be perfectly safe. You have always been his friend, even when he didn't deserve one."

"Whose friend?" Matthew swallowed hard. A splinter personality? Did Oskar know about this?

"Jeff's of course. He considers you a good friend despite all your flaws, your fears, your desire for revenge. That's the only part that concerns me. This need you have to see justice done."

A bobbing circle of light formed on the carpet in the hallway outside of the office door.

"Why are you here?" Matthew called out.

Jeff-Jack laughed. "To make a child's fondest

dream come true. Danny wants to live with you. He loves his Uncle Matt. Jeff saw it, I saw it. And if that bitch thinks she's going to drag him back with her, she's got another thing coming. You've had too many people run out on you—your father, your mother, your sister. This is the first time I've seen you come alive and it's because of Danny. I won't let her take him away. You deserve some happiness.''

He's after Jill. Matthew's heart threatened to burst out of his chest. What could he do? Would ''Jack'' listen to reason? He blurted out the first thing that came to him. ''I don't want Danny here. He's a nice kid and all, but I don't love him or anything like that,'' he stated, knowing in his heart it was a lie of the first order.

A large figure loomed in the doorway, the flashlight beam darting around the room, along bookcases, lingering in the corners, across the desk. Matthew stayed perfectly still, holding the lamp in one hand and the paperweight in the other.

''Jack's'' growl disappeared and Jeff's voice emerged. ''Really? You really don't like the kid that much?''

What? He was Jeff, now? But for how long? Matthew knew he had to act quickly, to take a chance and reason with a friend. Who knew how long they had until Jack emerged again? He had to act as if nothing unusual was happening and he couldn't do that from beneath the desk. He had to appear as if he weren't afraid of his old friend, that this was just one of their normal discussions....

Matthew unfolded himself from his hiding place, placing the lamp on the desk, but keeping the paperweight in his hand. He reached into his reporter's bag of tricks and found a halfway believable smile. "Naw…Danny's a decent kid, but I'm not ready for that type of responsibility." He tried to sound as lackadaisical as possible. "Let her take him. It's okay with me."

"Oh, well…" The lights suddenly flared back to life, temporarily blinding Matthew. He braced, half expecting an attack of some sort. As he grew more accustomed to the lights, he saw Jeff, in full combat regalia, camouflage fatigues, face paint and some sort of goggles pushed to the top of his head. At Jeff's feet was a duffel bag, which had a couple of road flares stuck in an end pocket.

Was it Matthew's imagination or did Jeff look smaller than before, less rigid, less threatening? Unless his zipped bag contained a weapon, Jeff carried nothing more lethal than a large flashlight in one hand and a small gadget in the other that resembled a garage door opener.

Jeff held the gadget up for Matthew's inspection. "Neat, eh? It's a remote control for your circuit breaker. On, off—" the electricity shut off and with it the lights "—and on again." The lights flared brightly again, even before they had a chance to dim completely.

"That's pretty useful." Matthew stepped closer, suddenly aware of the large knife strapped to Jeff's left leg—a knife with an odd serrated bladed. "Can I see it?"

Jeff grinned beneath his war paint. "Sure, buddy. It's really simple to do. It works off of a specific FM frequency and you—"

Matthew jumped him, managing to knock the remote control so that it flew backward toward the hall-way.

"Damn you!" Jeff roared in Jack's ominous growl.

They punched and kicked, Jeff trying to reach his knife and Matthew trying furiously to prevent him. Matthew might have been able to take Jeff two out of three falls, but Jack was another matter. Using a surprising amount of strength, cunning and a honed ability that Matthew never anticipated, Jack overpowered Matthew in a relatively short period of time.

He had the blade at Matthew's throat. "Tell her to come out," he whispered in his hoarse growl, "but to make Danny stay where he is. I don't want him to see this."

"You…screwed up last…time," Matthew said between gritted teeth. "He saw his father's body."

Jeff-Jack dug the tip of blade into Matthew's skin and a warm trickle of blood dripped down the front of his shirt. "And I won't make that mistake this time. Call her but make her leave Danny where he is!" He twisted Matthew's arm. "And if you say anything that warns her…"

Matthew coughed, stalling. Jeff-Jack gave his arm another warning twist. Matthew tried to sound as unconcerned as he could, praying she'd remember his careful instructions. He called out in a loud voice, "Uh…Jill, everything's okay, but I need for you to come see something. Tell Danny to stay put, okay?"

"Very convincing," Jack-Jeff purred in his ear. "Jeff was right. You do care a lot for the kid." He cocked his head. "I don't hear her."

"Sure you do." They both heard a scraping noise which Matthew knew was the sound of the bathroom window opening. "That's the closet door. She's coming now."

Jack-Jeff turned slightly toward the hallway. Matthew glanced out the window where he thought he saw a rustling in the shrubbery outside. It shook once, then twice. Jill and Danny were definitely escaping.

Releasing the breath he'd been holding, Matthew struggled to keep his tone light and conversational. "Hey, Jill, look who came to visit. It's Jeff—" He jerked one arm free and wedged it between Jack-Jeff's knife hand and his neck, moving the blade several important inches away from his throat. He kicked at the duffel bag, sending it across the room where its contents might not be as easily used against him and then he turned around in Jeff's weakened grasp and head-butted him.

As Jeff reeled from the blow, Matthew knocked his goggles loose, then spun out of his grasp, escaping toward the hallway. His first step to freedom landed on the remote control which crushed beneath his weight, plunging them into total darkness, and causing him to crash into the wall of the hallway. Jeff howled like a wounded dog, charging after him and tackling him.

Jack again proved his superior strength and ability, knocking Matthew nearly unconscious and dragging him back into the office.

"You'll sit here—" he tossed Matthew in his desk chair "—and you'll answer some questions. Understand, soldier?"

Matthew said nothing and a hand cuffed him in the temple.

"I said, understand, soldier?"

Matthew made a rude gesture which in the cover of

darkness, shouldn't have been visible, but he received a slap of admonition.

"I'll stand for no obscenities. Do you understand, soldier?" Jeff-Jack barked.

"Yes...sir," Matthew croaked. He had his answer; Jeff could see his gesture because he was wearing his goggles, night vision goggles that used infrared to literally see in the dark. In effect, Jeff could see Matthew, but Matthew couldn't see him.

"Where is the woman?" Jeff barked.

"Gone."

"No, she's not." Jeff caught him off guard with another blow to the head. "I've been watching the place. She's still here with the boy."

Matthew waited until he regained his senses before he spoke. "We had a prearranged code word to signal an all clear. I didn't give it so she knew to run. She and the boy have already reached a neighbor's house by now." He softened his voice, hoping to reach the side of Jeff that he had known for years. "It's over, Jeff. The police are on their way. Make it easy on yourself and give up."

Jeff-Jack laughed. "No, Jeff is tucked away someplace deep where he won't get out. He's too weak. But he's right about doing what's right for the child. Danny needs a man in his life. His father was useless, a poor excuse for a man. His death was mandatory."

"What about Carol?"

"An unfortunate bystander. She should have never been in his bed but sleeping on the couch like usual. It was her fault she put herself in harm's way."

"What about the others? I can understand Bummpt and the clown, even Thunder and Lightning, but why

Chandler and Miss Robinson? They were good people.''

"I told you," he thundered. "I do what's good for the children. Even the innocuous must step aside for the good of the children."

Matthew gave it one last try. "But how can it be good to make Danny an orphan?"

Jeff-Jack released a heavy sigh. "It's not for his good, it's for yours. For the good of the children. For the good of the child. For the good of Matthew Childs…"

There was no reasoning with a madman. To attempt to do so was an exercise in futility. But he had to stall Jeff, keep him in the house until the police could come.

They *were* coming, weren't they?

"Why are you here, Jack?"

Jeff-Jack backhanded him with increased fury. "How many times must I repeat myself?"

"No, not why you're here in my house. Why are you in Jeff's life? What did he lack in his life that made him need you?"

"His father." Jeff-Jack spat the word with derision. "He didn't see Jeff as a son but as a walking billboard for his practice. The doctor's son couldn't suffer from normal childhood trauma. The doctor's son couldn't be afraid of thunder or lightning or monsters under his bed or things that went bump in the night." His voice rose to a high screech. "The doctor's son couldn't be afraid of the dark. But I was."

Matthew noticed the sudden switch to first person. Jeff had slipped out for the moment.

"I was always afraid of the dark, but Dad said it was a childish fear and I had to deal with the situation with logic because I was so smart." He began to cry. "I hated being smart. I hated having a high IQ and being paraded around as Dad's pet project. I only wanted to be his son. But now Dad's going blind and when I get older, I'll go blind, too. I'll never be able to escape from the dark...."

As much as Matthew regretted taking advantage of Jeff in such an emotional state, this was the time to act. Now if only he could remember where the lamp was....

He leaned toward the desk, cringing in anticipation of another blow. But it didn't come. Jeff was muttering, evidently not paying close attention to him. Matthew reached out tentatively, feeling the edge of the desk with his fingertips. Finding the lamp's electrical cord, he followed it until he ran into the weighted base which contained the switch.

The lamp.

He lifted it slowly. "If it helps any, I'll admit I was scared of your father."

Jeff sniffed. "You, too? But I thought you liked him."

Matthew lied easily. "I never understood him. I never understood why he gave me this." He held up the lamp, hoping Jeff was looking at it.

"Put the lamp down." The voice became a growl again, accompanied by the unmistakable sound of a gun being cocked.

"Don't do anything hasty." Matthew lowered the lamp slowly. "I'm putting it down, see?" On that word, he switched on the lamp, knowing the sudden appearance of light would be magnified to painful proportions by the night vision goggles.

Jeff screamed in pain and used his gun hand to bat

at the light and the other to rip his goggles off and fling them across the room. "No fair!" he bellowed, like an injured child. "You play dirty, Matt!"

Matthew tackled him, knocking him over backward. They landed together on the floor, a tangle of arms and legs, each trying to gain control of the gun. Matthew punched, bit, clawed and everything else he could think to do to get the gun out of Jeff's hands. He could wait until another time to be appalled at his animalistic nature; at the moment, survival was the key.

In the end, Jeff proved to have the better training, having surprised Matthew by hooking a foot around his leg and pulling him off balance. Matthew fell backward and landed hard, seeing stars for a moment. As his vision cleared, the lone source of light, the lamp, swung from its cord off the edge of the desk, creating sweeping shadows as it cut a lazy arc through the air.

Matthew focused on the figure looming above him. The light danced back and forth over Jeff's face, highlighting different angles, as if he were vacillating between his two different personalities. But it was Jack in control, judging how he held the gun in steady hands, aiming at Matthew's head.

"You're going to die for that."

"No!"

Both voices emanated from one source: the man standing in front of Matthew, literally arguing with himself.

The gun lowered a couple of inches. "You can't kill Matt."

"The hell I can." The barrel snapped back up into position. "He's betrayed us. He made sure the woman escaped and sent her to call the authorities. That sort of treachery must be destroyed.''

"I will not let you kill my friend.'' Jeff looked at him with a sense of compassion that Matthew never knew him capable of possessing. The gun dropped a few more inches than before. "He's like my brother. We grew up together.''

"You mean your father preferred him to you. You've always resented Matthew because he was a grander demonstration of your father's healing qualities.'' Jack sneered and sighted the gun on Matthew's head. "Doc Oskar took a broken child and patched him up again. Well, see if he can patch up his star pupil this time!''

Two things happened simultaneously. Matthew dived forward, hoping Jack hadn't anticipated a moving target. As he leapt, he managed to snag the lamp which hung by the desk. But before the cord reached its full length and pulled out of the backup's outlet, he saw Jill appear in the doorway, holding a flashlight and what looked like a gun in her hands.

The lamp landed on him, the weighted base slamming into his head with enough force to stun him for a moment. But even stunned, he recognized the next sound, that of a gun being fired.

As something heavy fell across him, pinning him to the floor, he heard the faraway voice of Jill, calling his name. When he shook some sense back into his head, he realized he was beneath Jeff's inert body.

"Are you all right? Did he hit you?'' Her hands full, Jill pushed Jeff's body with her foot, trying to help free Matthew from the dead weight.

Matthew pushed to his knees and crawled over to

the man who had been his friend. Jeff now had a neat hole in his left temple.

And suddenly Matthew knew...

Jeff had remained his friend to the end.

"Is he...dead?"

Matthew nodded. "Yes."

"I heard him talking in two voices. I knew he was sick and then I realized how much danger you were in." She looked down and realizing she still had the gun, gently laid it on the desk. The beam of light from her flashlight started to shake and Matthew realized it was because her hands were shaking.

"I shot him," she whispered in dread. "I shot a man...."

Matthew stood up and put his hands on her shoulders as much to calm her as to brace himself. "No, you didn't. He shot himself. Jeff couldn't let Jack kill me."

"Jack?"

"His other personality. The one who killed Bummpt and the others. You were right. He was doing it for the good of the children." He straightened. "Where's Danny?"

"At your neighbor's house. We called the police, then I came back. I found the policeman in the bushes and I took his gun and came in. I couldn't let you face...him alone."

Matthew looked at Jeff's lifeless body, the bright red pool of blood on the floor. Real blood. Not the inky stuff in grainy black-and-white photos.

"I wasn't alone. I had my friend Jeff with me."

And then Matthew started crying.

Epilogue

Six months later

"There's no one in the closet, Danny, I checked."

Danny pulled the covers up to his lip which stuck out farther than usual. "What about under the bed?"

Matthew knelt and spotted today's socks and shirt nestled among the dust bunnies. "Absolutely nothing under there except for some dirty clothes. You'll pick those up in the morning."

"Well..." Danny thought it over and finally seemed satisfied. "Okay. No bogeymen, tonight."

Matthew still flinched internally when Danny used that word. It was almost as if he had decided that the best way to disarm the past was to give it new meaning. Today's bogeyman liked to reach out of hiding places and do nothing more dangerous than pinch toes.

"Good." Matthew reached down and playfully pinched Danny's toe through the blanket. "Your toes are safe for one more night. Good night, sport."

"Good night, Uncle—" He stopped and a look of puzzlement filled his face. "You aren't my uncle."

Matthew shrugged. "Technically, no."

"What's tech'ly mean?"

He sighed. Another definition. Danny had been on a definition kick for the last month. At this rate, by the time he reached first grade, he was going to have a vocabulary befitting a college freshman. "It means after what we've gone through today, I guess I'm not just your uncle anymore."

"You're my...what is it called?"

"Stepfather," Matthew replied, giving Danny's blanket the final tuck.

Danny contemplated that bit of news by closing one eye in heavy concentration. "Then, can I call you Daddy?"

Matthew felt a flutter in his stomach. "Sure. In fact, I think I'd like it a lot."

Danny's response was a sleepy yawn. "Okay. G'night, Daddy." For Matthew, it was the adoption of an awesome responsibility. For Danny? Merely a change in terminology.

"Good night...son." *Son.* It felt good. Damned good. Jill was going to flip when he told her this. They'd been worried about how Danny would adapt to this new life they were going to share. Looks like they worried for nothing....

Matthew headed out the door, then paused, remembering why Danny had called him in the first place. "Danny, you want a night-light, tonight? Your mom brought one."

Danny templed his fingers, looking all the world like a little old man. "Well...I guess not. I'm not 'fraid of the dark."

"Okay." He switched off the overhead, plunging the room into pitch-blackness. "But, Danny?"

"Yes, Daddy?"

"It's okay if you're afraid of the dark. You can

always tell your mom or me if you're scared about anything. Okay, sport?''

The little voice sounded strong and secure. ''I know, Daddy. Good night.'' There was a moment's hesitation. ''I love you, Daddy.''

''And I love you, Danny.''

They both released satisfied sighs in the dark.